WREAKING HAVOC

INTERNATIONAL BESTSELLING AUTHOR
HARLEY STONE

For Meltarrus: my Havoc, my peace, my lover, and my best friend who pushes me to challenge boundaries, break rules, and who calms the raging bitch inside me. Thank you for always believing in me and encouraging me to follow my heart. I couldn't do any of this without you. I love you!

INTRODUCTION

She's a recovering mean girl who needs a formidable date. He has anger issues and a heart of gold. Together, they could either destroy the world or save it.

Fresh out of jail, the Dead Presidents MC Sargent at Arms, Marcus "Havoc" Wilson, is trying to lay low and keep his PTSD-induced temper under control while helping other military veterans rejoin society. In search of relaxation techniques, Havoc stumbles upon an alluring bookstore owner with a violent past of her own who's able to calm him down in ways he's never experienced.

Julia Edwards gave up her life of privilege the minute she tried to kill her ex-husband, and she doesn't want it—or him—back. As a small Seattle bookstore owner, she's determined to spend her days hidden between the covers of romance novels until her real-life fantasy appears and shakes up her entire existence.

Introduction

Can these two attempted murderers find peace together? Or will the loose ends from their pasts unravel their future?

PROLOGUE

Havoc

Three Months Ago

SEATTLE DRIVERS ARE assholes. Our traffic jams are legendary, and today, 5th Avenue is a parking lot. By five-thirty p.m. it was already getting dark and the normal January drizzle had started up again, screwing with visibility and slopping up the roads. Then, some narcissistic motherfucker in a Mercedes decided he was too important to wait, made an illegal turn, squeezed in front of a minivan, and almost clipped my bike.

The asshole probably didn't even see me since he was staring at his phone the entire time. Thankfully, I saw him and swerved my Fatboy out of the way, coming within inches of a parked car in the process.

He had the gall to honk at me. At me! Like I'd almost run *him* over. Maybe he thought I didn't deserve to be on the road because I was driving a

Harley instead of a Mercedes? Who knew how the minds of rich, entitled motherfuckers worked? Since there wasn't a damn place to go, he came to an abrupt stop. I squeezed my bike between him and a parked car and knocked on his window.

Looking at me like I wasn't worth the air I was breathing, he rolled his window down half an inch like a fucking coward.

"Didn't get very far, did you, asshole?" I asked.

"Fuck you," he said and rolled up his window.

It would be so easy to rip my helmet off and use it to bash in the side of his car. Rewarding, even. At least for a couple of minutes. Then the guilt would set in as I remembered how goddamn hard I'd worked to not be the man who flew off the handle anymore. I'd gained a lot of ground over the past few years, and I would not let some pansy-ass bitch-boy make me lose it.

"He's not worth it."

They weren't my words, but Sage, the Dead Presidents Motorcycle Club's counselor, had drilled them into my head. Most clubs didn't have counselors, but when you shove a ragtag bunch of military vets with post-traumatic stress disorder together, a counselor is necessary. Believe that.

Sage would also tell me to take a beat and chill the fuck out. That sounded like a good plan, so I parked my bike, fed the meter, and scanned the area for some place I could cool my heels. A bar named The Line sat in the middle of the next block. Determined to take five and not let some entitled asshole get the best of me, I hoofed it down the street and slipped inside the bar.

Sports paraphernalia was plastered all over the walls and the basketball game was on. I got a couple of sideways looks, but nothing I wasn't used to, especially while wearing my cut. Confident I'd found a watering hole I could somewhat relax in, I pulled up a barstool and ordered a stout.

The game was a close one, stressing me out far more than it should have, but if the Blazers didn't get their shit together, they'd be out of the playoffs again. They missed two free-throws, and I shook my head and went out back to smoke.

I was just about to light up when I heard the muffled cry of a girl.

The city was loud, but I knew what I'd heard. Straining my ears, I put my smokes back in my pocket and ventured out into the covered picnic area.

"Don't you fuckin' bite me, you little whore," a male voice said.

There was a loud slap, and the woman called out again. Grunting followed.

I rounded the divider to find some wiry asshole plowing into a girl bent over a picnic table. He had one hand covering her mouth while the other held her down. She met my gaze, and her eyes begged me to intervene.

Her attacker was so busy rutting into her he didn't see me. I crept around behind him, grabbed him by the back of his shirt, and hauled his ass off her, holding him inches above the ground as his little pencil dick jutted outward.

"I see why you can't get women the right way, but this shit ain't gonna fly," I growled.

"What the fuck are you doing?" he asked, helicoptering his hands to swing at me. "Let me go! This is none of your business."

The girl was crying. I couldn't see enough to make out her features, but I could hear the sobs pouring out of her. He'd been fucking raping her while she bawled. Rage boiled up, threatening to consume me.

"Let me go!" he demanded again. "You fuckin' lawn jockey."

That did it. My vision blurred around the edges and my breathing deepened. I set him down and wound up. My right hook to his jaw resulted in a satisfying crunch. Now he was screaming, which sounded much better than listening to his victim cry. Left hook to the gut, another crunch. Probably a rib. Maybe two. He tried to block me, and I snapped his arm.

"Ahhh what the fuck, man?"

I was too far gone to respond. I dropped him and he spun around, giving me the perfect shot at his left kidney. Bam! Bet the motherfucker didn't expect that. He fell to the ground and I went with him, my vision exploding in red.

The next thing I knew, men were hauling me off him and trying to contain me. Sirens closed in on us. Lights flashed. I was in handcuffs and being read my rights. They pulled me out front and stuffed me into the backseat of a cruiser. Looking over my shoulder one last time, I saw the girl being loaded into an ambulance. She'd be okay. That made it all worth it.

I knew the drill, so I kept my mouth shut

4

through all the questions and threats until the boys in blue let me have my one phone call.

Dialing Link, my club president and closest friend, I rested my forehead against the wall and waited for him to pick up.

He accepted the collect call, like I knew he would.

"Havoc? What's going on?"

"I'm in jail, brother. I fucked up. But this time, I swear to you, the bastard deserved it."

1

Julia

Present Day

MY LITTLE SISTER, Laura, stood in the doorway of my bathroom, watching me darken my lashes and color my lips. With blonde hair and pale blue eyes, she looked like the female version of our father. But where he was serious and handsome, she was a jovial beauty with an easy smile and carefree nature that made people gravitate toward her. She pulled people in, and I did my best to repel them. As the recipient of Mom's fiery red hair, intense green eyes, and savage resting bitch face, I couldn't pull off beautiful or innocent. But strikingly terrifying... I had that shit down.

And because I was a contouring wizard, I could paint myself into something more approachable when the situation required it. Luckily, few situations did. Brushing my newest purchase—a shade of blush called 'Party Girl'—on my cheek, I frowned. "Too pink."

Laura nodded. "Scoot over and let me try it," she said, joining me in front of the mirror.

I passed her the new blush, wiped the pink crap off, and went back to the earthier tone I normally wore. Laura being in my space felt comfortable now, but it hadn't always been that way between us. In fact, I could pinpoint the exact moment she became more than the annoying baby sister who stole my clothes and makeup and narked to my parents when I ditched her at the mall. It happened about ten years ago in front of a different bathroom mirror.

I was preparing for my first day of college and Laura was about to head to her high school freshman orientation. She stood at my bathroom doorway watching me work then, too.

Nervous about being a little fish on a big campus where people didn't automatically know and fear me and my family, I didn't have the time or energy to deal with the brat, so I cut her an annoyed look and asked, "Can I help you?"

Normally so damn bubbly and sweet she gave me a freaking toothache, that day Laura looked somber and subdued. I'd never seen her like that, and it made me uncomfortable. She stepped into the bathroom, nodding. "I... I have a zit." Turning her head to the side and brushing her hair back, she revealed the bright red blemish taking up the lower quarter of her cheek. "You're really amazing at makeup. Will you please show me how to hide it?"

I considered her predicament for a solid ten seconds while my inner bitch reveled in her misery. After all the times she'd stolen my makeup, this felt like karma. And who was I to question karma? But, she was also my little sister, and therefore a reflection on me. I couldn't let her begin high school sporting such a heinous imperfection. Pointing at the toilet, I said, "Sit."

A smile lit up her face as she skittered over to the toilet, sat, and looked up at me expectantly. I opened the top drawer of my bathroom vanity and started pulling out products. As I went to work evening out her skin tone and contouring away the swelling, I gave her a mini tutorial, explaining the purpose and use for each product.

When I finished, she stood in front of the mirror, sweeping back her hair. "I can't even see it anymore. That's... that's incredible." She met my gaze in the mirror, her eyes glistening. "Thank you, Julia. You're like the best sister ever."

I wasn't, but her praise made me feel more warm and fuzzy than I'd ever admit.

"You're not as bitchy as everyone says you are."

By everyone, she meant our peers. The children of Seattle's filthy rich and terrifyingly powerful (kind of like the Illuminati, but localized and more devious). They built, and they destroyed. I knew, because I was their star pupil, their protégé, their sword. Laura and our peers had no idea how bitchy I could be. I was learning to pull strings, play friends against each other, manipulate the results. I was learning to play the game, and I fucking loved it.

But I never let my little sister see that side of me.

And years later, when karma came knocking, Laura was the one person who warned me to check the peep hole before I opened the door.

I would do anything for my sister.

"Keep the blush. It looks better on you," I said, smiling at her in the mirror.

She grinned, her dimples making her look fourteen again instead of twenty-four as she closed the compact and slipped it into her purse. "It really does. Thanks."

But she was still a snarky little brat.

I straightened and took one last look in the mirror. "Let's do this."

Laura pushed off the counter. "I'm so beyond ready to be pampered. Wedding planning is stressful."

Sure. Like Mom would actually allow Laura to plan anything. My sister was just another piece in our parents' game. And now, with her nuptials less than a week away, we needed to hit the spa so we could look our best for the upcoming festivities. God forbid we attend a bridal shower or a bachelorette party with imperfect nails, faded highlights, or unsightly body hair.

Some things simply were not done.

Especially not if you were an Edwards. We'd spent our entire lives conforming to the image of perfection demanded by our family name and status, and although I'd turned out to be a tremendous disappointment, Laura was still going strong. I didn't agree with her commitment to the cause, but I supported her and would do what I could to help.

"Have you decided on a plus-one for the wedding yet?" she asked, her tone light and conversational with a tiny hint of panic.

I understood her worry, because every time I so

much as thought about attending her wedding, my chest would squeeze, my eyes would burn, and I'd break out in cold sweats. Giving myself a much-needed moment to respond, I locked up my condo and slid the keys into my purse.

"Not yet. Has Wesley RSVP'd?"

Wesley. There were too many emotions wrapped up in that one name. He'd been my husband, my partner, and now he was dead to me. Too bad he was still very much alive to my family.

Laura nodded, looking away.

My stomach sank. "Who's he bringing?"

"Jozette."

The rage I'd been working so diligently to keep bottled, bubbled to the surface, blurring my vision and making the world sway. Leaning against the wall, I took a couple of deep breaths and counted to ten. Jozette West had been my friend since grade school. We'd co-chaired committees together in high school. She'd been my college roommate and one of the six bridesmaids at my wedding. She was weak and untrained, and I could crush her. I could make her regret ever betraying me.

But I was out of the game and didn't want to be that person anymore.

"I'm sorry, Julia."

Swallowing back pain and anger, I pushed off the wall. Hoping Laura would drop the subject and give me a moment to breathe, I led her down the stairs.

"Michael said Joel doesn't have a date yet, and he'd love to accompany you."

She didn't know when to give up. Although I understood and appreciated her need to be helpful, my pride wouldn't allow me to accept a pity date with the friend of my little sister's fiancé.

"No."

She grabbed my arm and tugged, turning me around to face her. She stood on the step above me, giving herself a rare height advantage. "Joel's a really nice guy. Nothing at all like Wesley. He's always had a crush on you. You should give him a chance."

"I can't, Em. He's part of the circle."

She threw her hands in the air. "You talk about us like we're some kind of cult."

Cults weren't usually as resourceful or dangerous. I didn't need a date for Laura's wedding; I needed a shield to hide me from prying eyes and whispering voices, so I could survive the event without going nuclear. He had to be handsome, loyal, fearless, and ferocious, and I was pretty sure men like that had gone extinct.

"I'll find a date."

Finished with the conversation, I rushed the rest of the way down the stairs and made my way through the small, cramped bookstore I owned and managed named One More Chapter. The smell of books greeted me, calming me down like a drug. I took in a hit through my nose and felt my shoulders relax as I made a mental note of the elderly couple browsing the westerns section.

"You heading out?" My assistant, Justine, asked without looking up from one of the many thick textbooks piled on the counter in front of her. As a first-year pre-med student at Seattle Pacific, her coursework was the stuff of nightmares. She'd come into the bookstore about six months ago, searching for the type of part-time employment that would allow her to collect a paycheck while she studied. I didn't really need the help, but she was from a middle-class family and needed the money, and I enjoyed the company and freedom her presence allotted.

"Yep," Laura said with a smile. "I'll have her back in time to lock up."

"An order should come in soon," I said, dragging my feet. "Some new releases, so check the dates to make sure you can put them out. If you have any questions, you know how to reach me."

Still not taking her eyes off her textbook, Justine waved me off. "Go. Have fun. I've got this."

When I didn't immediately run out the door, Laura grabbed my hand and dragged me to the double-parked Town Car waiting for us. A gray-haired man wearing a suit sprang from the driver's seat and hurried around to open the back door for us.

"Hi Franck," I said, greeting him as I slid in.

"Ms. Edwards." He nodded. "Nice to see you again."

Franck was French, since all uppity families should have at least one French employee. A kind widower in his late sixties with an amiable smile and a mischievous twinkle in his eye, he mostly drove for my family, but also sometimes filled in for the butler. Although he was loyal to my parents, he practiced discretion and didn't tattle unless directly asked. When I was young, he'd patiently retrieved me from several places I shouldn't have been, telling as little as possible to my parents. I liked to think I added a little excitement to Franck's otherwise boring job.

"Will you be heading to the club for your spa day?" he asked.

Along with the rest of Seattle's rich and snobby, my family frequented a country club on Bainbridge Island. Despite their world-famous golf course, fantastic spa, and attentive staff, my sister's wedding would be the one and only time I returned to the club.

"No," I said, settling in my seat. "Laura has reluctantly agreed to go slumming with me at the spa on the corner of Pine and Fourth."

He grinned. "How very kind of her."

Laura climbed in, scowling at us both. "Indeed. I should probably get nominated for sainthood for this."

"Noted. Immediately following your wedding, I will send a request to the Pope."

Franck chuckled and returned to his seat.

Twisting in my seat to face my sister, I asked, "Speaking of the wedding, how's the seating chart coming?"

"Good. Mom finished it last night. Since Mayor Kinlan's family won't be able to attend, she invited the Cowleys."

"I can't believe the drama going down with the Kinlans. I'm too busy to follow the gossip, but I've seen the headlines. Everyone must feel *so* scandalized." I rolled my eyes to show her exactly how I felt about Seattle's ex-Mayor Kinlan and his son, Noah, who had recently been convicted of an extensive list of crimes ranging from tax evasion to sex trafficking.

Everyone knew the top one-percent skirted the law, but the sex trafficking had been a surprise. That was taking influence and privilege a bit too far. Still, it would be strange not seeing them at the wedding. There were two things you could count on during any high society social event. My great aunt, Martha, would get plastered and flirt with the young, attractive male servers, and Mayor Kinlan could be found schmoozing his loyal followers and fishing for campaign contributions.

"Scandalized," she asked, eyeing me like I had said something wrong. "Don't you think you're being a little heartless?"

I blinked. "No?"

"The Kinlans are dead, Julia."

Certain I must have misheard her, I asked, "What?"

"You haven't heard?" she asked.

"No. Last I'd heard they were on trial and the evidence was mounting against them. I haven't picked up a paper in a few days."

"Yesterday morning they were found hanging in their jail cells."

"Like some sort of double suicide? They don't seem like the type." I'd already tugged my phone from my purse and was thumbing it on to search the internet for details.

A picture of Emily Stafford popped up. She was the attorney who'd taken the case defending the biker accused of beating the shit out of Noah. I'd met Emily Stafford at a charity dinner. She tried to speak to me while we were waiting for our coats, but that was back when I was a card-carrying entitled bitch, and she wasn't the type of person I wanted to be seen with. I'd ignored her and walked off while she was mid-sentence. Not my best moment. Not my worst, either.

I kept scanning articles until I found information on the hangings. "Says here they used their pants to create the ropes to hang themselves."

"To hang *themselves*?" Laura's eyes widened as she glanced toward the front of the car and leaned toward me, lowering her voice. "I'm not supposed to talk about it, but everyone is saying they were murdered."

Murdered sounded a lot more realistic than some sort of father-son suicide pact, but... "In jail?" I asked, still skeptical.

She nodded.

Our parents rarely encouraged Laura to discuss anything related to the community's power plays. My sister wasn't stupid, but she was innocent and naïve, and sometimes she stumbled across truths she couldn't handle. Truths that could get her in trouble if she voiced them in front of the wrong person. Thankfully, she usually came to me with her ideas, and I'd gotten great at derailing them before she sped into dangerous territory. Laura was the type of person to be protected, shielded, not involved. I held up a hand, preparing to once again lead her down a safer path. "This sounds like another one of your crazy conspiracy theories."

Hurt flashed across her eyes, making me feel like a total bitch. "There are rumors they were talking about a deal. About rolling over on someone to get their sentences reduced."

"That usually happens before the trial," I pointed out.

She sighed, frowning. "I know you don't care about the gossip anymore, but you should keep reading." She gestured at the phone in my lap. "There's a lot of shady stuff going on."

I couldn't care less about the lives of my old peers, but their deaths... and Laura's insistence that foul play was involved... that interested me. Besides, the side-eye look she was giving me promised she wouldn't let up until I complied. Rolling my eyes like it was a bother, I continued to scan the articles. My gaze stopped when it landed on a head shot of the biker who'd attacked Noah. Dark skin, shaved head, dark intelligent eyes, sexy, full beard, slight smirk gracing his plump lips, thick neck, broad shoulders, muscles on top of muscles. Damn, he was huge. He looked like a man who'd level a city if it got in his way. He was the exact opposite of my pale-skinned, blond-haired, blue-eyed, slender ex-sleaze bucket, and maybe that's why I couldn't take my eyes off him.

Hello, handsome.

"Hottie, isn't he?" Laura asked, leaning over my shoulder to see what had caught my attention.

I nodded, although 'hottie' didn't do him justice. More like sexy-as-hell. His slight smirk made promises that heated my blood and made my stomach flutter. My gaze dipped to his name. Marcus "Havoc" Wilson.

"Think I just found a date for your wedding," I said.

Her eyes widened. "A biker? One of *the bikers*

who helped with the Kinlan conviction? I bet Mom would just *love* that."

"You're only making him look more appealing."

She grabbed my phone and studied the photo, pulling out her own phone. "He's part of the Dead Presidents Motorcycle Club. This says they do a lot for the community, so I bet the number is listed." She punched in the information on her own phone. "Yep. Here it is. I'll send it to you."

My phone dinged with the incoming text and I rolled my eyes again.

"What?" she asked, smiling sweetly. "I'm trying to hook my big sister up for my wedding."

"I'm not calling a complete stranger and asking him out."

"Fine. Back to the seating chart," Laura said, growing suddenly somber. "You're at the family table. Across from Mom and Dad."

I threw back my head, bouncing it off the back of the seat. "Kill me now."

"It's the family table and you're family."

"Family would have told me about Wesley. They knew, and they kept it from me. Family doesn't do that. You're my only family."

"I know. They know. They're super sorry and it's been almost a year and they're hoping you'll forgive them."

Her claim held a major flaw. My parents never apologized for anything. "They're sorry, huh?"

"I'm sure they are. They miss you."

"And they said all of this?"

Her gaze drifted around the Town Car's interior, looking anywhere but at me. Such a horrible liar.

"You know how they are. They don't *say* things like that."

"God forbid someone think they're less than perfect."

"I know you're still angry, Julia, but this is my wedding. How would it look if my sister was sitting at the wrong table?"

The Edwards family appearances... that's what everything came down to. It might not matter to me anymore, but the family image was still important to Laura. I couldn't fault her for sipping the Kool-Aid when I'd gulped it down for years.

"Please do this for me," she begged.

"Fine."

She grinned, once again showing off her dimples. "You're the best sister ever."

There it was again, that heart-felt compliment that made me feel like shit. "Yeah, yeah."

She wiggled in her seat, letting out a little squeal. "I'm so excited! Can you believe my bachelorette party is tomorrow? I saw the RSVP list you sent. I know this isn't easy on you, and I appreciate all you've done."

My baby sister's special day was approaching, and I was her maid of honor. Thank god she had an amazing wedding coordinator, or nothing would have gotten done. All I'd done was show up for my dress fitting and put together her party RSVP list while dreading her big event. Best sister ever, indeed.

"I still can't believe I'm getting married!" she squealed again.

Despite my lack of faith in the sanctity of marriage, her enthusiasm was contagious. By the time Franck dropped us off, I was dreading her big day marginally less. Determined to put on my big girl panties and make it through the upcoming parties and ceremony with a smile, I hooked my arm in hers and we marched right into the spa to get pampered.

2

Havoc

'TRY GARDENING,' SHE said. *'It'll relax you,'* she promised.

Emily Stafford, the old lady and soon-to-be wife of my club president, Link, was a badass attorney. I owed her my freedom, but she didn't know shit about relaxation. As I stood on my front porch staring at a bed full of flowers in varying stages of death, I felt keyed-up and ready to kick the box to pieces.

I felt like a goddamn failure.

Here I was, ex-Army Special Forces Weapons Specialist, Sergeant at Arms for the Dead President's Motorcycle Club, I'd survived insane conditions and deadly terrain while dodging bullets, could keep an entire club of military veterans from killing each other, but couldn't keep a single flower alive. You'd think the time and money I'd blown on this so-called hobby would guarantee some measure of success, but no. The damn things were all determined to become compost.

Why the fuck?

Without a care for the nosy old couple across the street, I went to kick the box but pulled back at the last second, knowing if I started I wouldn't stop until nothing remained. And I wasn't about to lose my shit over goddamn flowers.

Yeah, gardening is fucking relaxing, Emily.

I should have thrown in the spade and given up, but it was about the principle now. Vegetation would not get the best of me. I had a fucking reputation to uphold. If I couldn't make these damn flowers survive, I'd just have to buy new ones every time Link and Emily came over.

And if that idea didn't make me sound batshit crazy...

While I sat there wondering how I could calm the fuck down from my "relaxing" hobby, Stocks pulled up on a custom orange and black Roadster. Born as Gage Sinclaire, I'd given Stocks his road name three months ago, when we'd met during my latest stint in the slammer. He was twenty-nine, and had spent nine years as a Marine Infantryman. Hell, from his clean buzz cut to his 'yes sir' attitude, he still looked and sounded like a soldier. He would have been a lifer in the service, but during a training exercise he'd lost one of his legs from the knee down, forcing him into retirement from his military career. With no idea what to do next, he took a friend's advice and became a certified financial advisor.

Which Stocks says is almost as stressful as gardening.

Stocks had a good head on his shoulders, but the action he'd seen gave him a case of PTSD significant enough that he had no business in a high-stress desk job handling the money of ungrateful, rich assholes. Like most veterans, he nutted up and hid his condition like a champ. At least until the market had a few too many down days and bitching clients wouldn't stop blowing up his phone and demanding that he move their money into safer investments. Stocks lost it and took his chair to the phone, computer, and security guys who'd tried to physically remove his out-of-control ass from the premises.

The minute I heard his story, I knew the Dead Presidents could help him escape society's expectations and become a man who could look himself in the mirror again. Just like the club had helped me. I signed up to sponsor him, and Link made him a prospect. Since Gage had lost his shit over stocks, landing him in the civilian version of the stockade, his road name was a given.

"Hey Brother," I said when he pulled off his helmet. "How's the bike workin' out for you?"

"Great." He grinned. "Feel like I'm really getting the hang of this shit."

Stocks had never ridden a sled before, so Wasp, the club's vice president, helped him find a used one and replaced enough parts to make it roadworthy. Then I'd taken Stocks and our bikes outside of Renton to teach him how to ride. The prosthetic leg had been tricky, but he'd managed. Now he had a motorcycle endorsement on his license, and judging by the grin currently stretched across his face, he'd discovered why the rest of us preferred sleds to cages. There was nothing in the world like the freedom of your bike on an open road. Especially for those of us who'd paid a price for that freedom.

His gaze drifted to the dead flowers in the box beside me and his smile fell. "Weren't those alive last night? What the hell happened?"

"Shit if I know." And I didn't want to discuss it. I threw one more disgusted look at my failure before standing. "You ready to head to the station?"

His grin returned, and he put his helmet back on.

Friday nights always begin with church, but tonight's weekly meeting felt different from normal. An air of excitement and anticipation floated above the pews in the old converted fire station now serving as club headquarters. Eagle, the club's secretary, rattled off the minutes from our last meeting. Everyone voted to approve them, then Specks, our treasurer, gave a run-down of the financials.

"Any old business?" Link asked, opening up the floor.

He waited a few beats, and when nobody spoke up, he stood and started pacing. "Now for new business. We have the homeless outreach coming up in two weeks, so we need to finalize some shit. Spade, have you talked to your uncle about donations?"

Spade, whose uncle owned one of the local

restaurants, nodded. "Yessir. He said he'll donate hamburgers and hot dogs again."

"Please give him our thanks. He's a good man."

Spade nodded again.

"Anyone else able to secure a donation?" Link asked.

Stocks raised his hand. "The firm I used to work for said they'll pitch in bottled waters."

Link smiled. "Thanks, brother."

Sage stood. "My office will get the buns."

"Great," Link said, turning to Flint, the manager of the Copper Penny which was the bar and grill run by the Dead Presidents. "The restaurant will provide the sides."

Flint nodded. "I'll get them ordered, Prez."

"All right." Link clapped his hands together. "Last time we did this, we fed about two hundred homeless, so we're gonna need some bodies. Girlfriends, parents, kids, whoever wants to show up and help us serve, is welcome. I'll need you all here to mingle and find out who was in the service and who wasn't."

"Is this really necessary, Prez?" a brother named Zombie asked. "I mean, it's good that we help the community, but last time we did one of these, we had homeless people coming around for days, looking for another handout."

Link dropped his head and paced the front of the room. Those who didn't know him would assume he was considering the question, but I knew Link better than that. Our president was preparing an argument. He was a wise man who liked to get the details worked out before he opened his mouth.

"A lot of the vets on the streets are there because they choose to be," Zombie continued. "Strung out on drugs or crazy as fuck... we can't do anything about that shit. Sometimes it seems like we're wasting our time and resources... spinin' our wheels when we could be doing something more worthwhile."

"That's a valid concern," Link admitted. "Thanks for voicing it. Thing is... that, right there is exactly why we have to continue."

Zombie's brow furrowed.

"What you said just now. I've heard it a thousand times. Who else in this room has heard those same arguments? 'Vets get more help than anyone.' 'Most homeless vets are on the streets because they're addicted to drugs or crazy as shit?' We've heard it all, haven't we?"

Nods of agreement and mutters of affirmation fluttered around the room.

"And how many of us—how many of the brothers here today—would be on the street in the same situation without this club? I can name seven of you who have abused morphine for pain management. Who here hasn't had a discussion with a doctor about triggers and received a prescription for fuckin' antidepressants, pain blockers, or antipsychotics? Shit, most of us could have easily ended up on the streets. But we didn't. Why? What's the one thing that separates us from them?"

"Each other," Wasp answered.

"Exactly," Link agreed. "I know if I fuck up, I have a club full of brothers who are going to call me to the carpet. These men on the street, they don't have that. They don't have Havoc to kick their asses and set them straight. Or Pops to nag their ear off and make them get back into line just to shut him up. No Sage to listen as they talk through the memories and nightmares fuckin' with their heads. The entire world looks at them and sees nothing but goddamn junkies and loonies, but we know better. We know what they've been through... what they've seen... and it's our duty to offer them a way out of the hell they continue to live in. That's why the Dead Presidents was founded, and it's why we continue to stay the fuckin' course. You feel me, Zombie?"

Zombie nodded.

"Anyone else have questions or concerns they'd like to bring to the table for discussion?" Link asked.

Nobody said shit.

"Any other new business?"

Link had new business. Our president was close to bursting at the seams to share his news. Hell, he'd already told me privately because he kept secrets like a goddamn school girl with her first crush. I couldn't fault him, though. Link was happier than I'd ever seen him, and it served as a testament to his leadership skills and patience that he hadn't blurted out the news the second we all arrived. Staying the course, following meeting protocol, he practiced what he preached.

Wasp, our vice president chuckled, hitting the table. "Shit, I'm just here for the party, Prez. Heard you might have a reason to celebrate you wanted to share with us."

As his name suggested, Wasp was a white, Anglo-Saxon Protestant, spawned from old money and raised in privilege. Despite his family's connections and wealth, he was a good-natured, level-headed, humble man. He'd served in the Navy as a boat mechanic, and as he put it, the only real danger he saw came from the slop the cooks served. He had no deep-seated issues or PTSD flare-ups, which meant that unlike most of us, he'd joined the Dead Presidents out of a want to help others, rather than a need to help himself.

Wasp was a good man, here to help other good men.

But he was also a smartass who liked to get under Link's skin. Despite that fact—or maybe even because of it—the three of us were closer than most biological brothers. No doubt Link had also shared his news with Wasp. Hell, half the club probably already knew by now. The announcement was merely a formality at this point.

"I'm getting there. Have some goddamn patience," Link growled, looking over the room as he waited for anyone else to speak up with new business. When nobody did, he announced, "I asked Emily to marry me."

The room filled with hoots, hollering, and congratulations. When the ruckus died down, Wasp hit the table to get Link's attention and said, "Aww man, she was about to leave your sorry ass for me."

"Not fuckin' likely. I already told you, stay the hell away from my woman. Goddamn pretty boy can't even find his own woman," Link grumbled.

"That hot little number agreed to marry your ugly ass?" Tank asked. Tank had been a tank driver back in the day... as in way back in the day. He was one of the founders who'd helped Link's dad form the Dead Presidents, making him one of Link's many honorary uncles.

Link flipped him off, grinning. "Yep. The day you drugged Amy and forced that ring on her finger I realized there's hope for every sorry motherfucker out there."

The room filled with laughter as Tank nodded, conceding the point.

Jake, Link's father and the original club president, stood, waving a beer in the air. "I move we wrap this shit up, so we can get to celebrating. My boy's getting married to a good woman who makes him happy, brothers. I couldn't be prouder. Now, maybe I'll get some damn grandkids before I die."

Loud cheers of agreement erupted, kicking off what promised to be a good time. One by one the men came up to congratulate Link. I stood back and watched as my friend shook hands and took an endless supply of shit from the rag-tag group of men he called family.

"Can't believe he's really doing it," Wasp said, sidling up to me. "They've known each other for, what? Three months?" He shook his head. "He's a braver man than me."

Link wasn't scared of anything. Not even marriage. "No balls, no babies," I agreed.

Wasp stared at me for a second before clapping my back, throwing back his head, and laughing. "No balls, no babies, indeed. Havoc, you are one quiet motherfucker, but sometimes when you say shit, you sound like a goddamn biker Yoda. Come on.

Let's go find Emily and see how many hugs we can steal from her before Link kicks our asses."

Watching Link and Wasp throw down was always amusing, so I followed Wasp out of the meeting room and into the common area where the women were waiting for us.

"Jesus," Wasp swore.

My gaze followed his until it landed on the crowd surrounding the old fire pole in the center of the room. Jayson, Emily's flamboyant assistant, was dressed in a flowing button-down teal shirt and black leather pants so tight I could see his religion, gyrating his hips against the pole as his hands stroked it reverently, like it was a giant cock. A circle consisting of old ladies and club whores surrounded him, watching with wide-eyed fascination and what looked a hell of a lot like curiosity. One woman held a notepad and pen and appeared to be taking notes.

The club whores wore close to nothing while the old ladies dressed a little more conservatively. Emily and her grandmother, Annabell, were part of the circle, but they stood out like a couple of Ducatis in a room full of Harleys. Even dressed down, they looked classier and more refined.

"Never a dull moment around that one," Wasp said with a chuckle, nodding in Jayson's direction.

Emily saw us and excused herself to wander over and give us each a hug. "How's the gardening coming along?" she asked, releasing me to accept another of Wasp's hugs, which the bastard held onto a little too long to be brotherly.

"Dead," Stocks piped in, joining us. "It's like a tomb where perfectly good flowers go to die."

"Really?" Emily asked. "What happened?"

I shrugged. "Watered them. They get sunlight. Even got them some of those plant food sticks. Seems like the more I do for them, the faster they die. Any suggestions?" I asked.

She shook her head. "Plants never live long around me. I usually forget about them until they're on the brink of death, then I water them just in time to save them. Yours at least get to die. My plants live in eternal purgatory. Maybe you should try a gardening book or something? There's a little bookstore a couple of blocks down on Eighth Avenue. I bet they have something that could help you."

"Or you could just give up," Wasp suggested. "You're more fun when you're beatin' the shit out of people. I don't think I like this anger-controlled pussy version of Havoc."

I gave him a little love tap, shoving him into the side of a pool table, reminding him that this 'anger-controlled pussy version' could still rearrange his face.

"Rude motherfucker," he said, laughing as he righted himself and rejoined us. "Here comes Link." Wasp snaked his arm across Emily's shoulders. "We gotta show him our love and make him jealous so he steps up his game. Can't have the prez goin' limp on you."

Emily elbowed Wasp in the side. "Trust me, that is *not* a problem Link has to worry about. Quit messing with my man, Wasp, or I'll pull out my taser and see how many volts you can take before you cry like a little bitch."

Rubbing his jaw, he looked her over before asking, "Can I cop a feel while I'm flailing? Because that would be worth it."

"You're impossible," she said, giving him one more elbow before joining Link.

"She wants me," Wasp said, watching her walk away.

If I thought for a moment he was serious, I'd kick his ass good for him, but I knew better. Despite his clowning, Wasp would do anything for Link. We all would. Tank's old lady offered me a beer, and I accepted, leaning against a pillar to watch Link wrap an arm around Emily. Jayson held up a glass of something pink and bubbly, making a toast that ended in, "Let's party, bitches," which made everyone cheer.

This was our little slice of heaven, and I felt content to bask in my friend's happiness, while wondering what it would be like to have someone look at me the way Emily looked at Link. I'd never had that in my life, never even wanted it. Before I could give much thought to my sudden curiosity, Eagle held up a dart and asked if I was up for a game.

3

Julia

SUNDAY MORNING, THE incessant buzzing of my alarm shot bolts of pain through my pounding head and reminded me I needed to get up and get my ass to work. Groaning and cursing last night's bad decisions, I turned off my alarm and cradled my head in my hand as I took in my surroundings. My apartment. I was alone, still in my clothes, and sprawled across my bed with my phone in hand.

Crap.

Praying I had done nothing stupid like drunk texting, I bolted to a seated position—wincing against the sharp pain brought on by the change of elevation—and checked my outgoing texts. Nothing. Sighing in relief, I opened my phone's windows to see exactly what I had been up to. Wesley's Instagram page popped up.

Like a loser, I'd been stalking my ex-husband's pictures. Awesome. And now I was curious, so I glanced through them again. Lots of pictures with different women hanging all over him like he was some sort of rock star. Stupid poser. Not even worth stalking. At least I hadn't texted him.

Bullet dodged, I massaged my temples and tried to remember what else I'd done last night. Fragmented scenes from a club on Pike Street flashed through my memory. Loud music, packed dance floor, fru-fru drink in hand. Determined to let loose and enjoy Laura's bachelorette party, I'd invented my own personal drinking game. Every time one of Laura's friends asked about Wesley, why they hadn't seen me at the country club, or who my date for the wedding would be, I excused myself to order another drink. I don't know how many times I visited the bar before they cut me off, but judging by my headache... too many. Enough to have no memory of getting home. Needing to make sure I hadn't made a complete ass of myself, I called Laura.

She answered with a sleepy, "Hello," followed by, "You're alive?"

"You sound surprised."

"I am," she admitted. "After the Jell-O shots, I fully expected you to be sleeping off one hell of a hangover. How do you feel?"

Like a person with no memory of Jell-O shots. Hopefully I hadn't taken them off someone's body. "Like death, but I must endure. I have a store to run, after all. Never underestimate the fortitude of the small business owner."

"Of course not, sis. Just be sure our fortuitous business owner is at the bridal shower by three."

Laura had a habit of misusing words. It was one

34

of her more endearing qualities. "You know fortitude and fortuitous don't mean the same thing,
right?"

"Whatever. Just be proud of me for using a big
word and be sure to look gorgeous by the shower.
Not too gorgeous, of course, since I'll want everyone's eyes on me, but gorgeous enough that I can
call you my sister without hanging my head in embarrassment."

"Of course, your highness." Purpose renewed, I
headed for the bathroom cabinet to grab something
for my headache. My image in the mirror was terrifying. Crazy bedhead, puffy eyes, makeup smudged
everywhere, I looked more suited for a horror flick
than a bridal shower. I needed to pull myself together and look presentable before I had to face my
mom, Wesley's mom, and the rest of the fake bitches
of Seattle's top one-percent.

Also, I was going to need more alcohol to get
through the day.

"How early is too early to drink?" I asked before
popping some ibuprofen into my mouth and
heading for the kitchen to start a pot of coffee. "I
mean mimosas and bloody marys are technically
breakfast food so is there really a designated start
time?"

Laura giggled. "I think you should stay away
from alcohol for a while. Give your liver a chance to
flush out all the crap you flooded it with last night.
By the way, how'd it go with the guy you took home?
Did you get lucky?"

I froze and recounted my steps. Had there been a
guy? No one was in my bed. Had he left early? Or

was there still a random stranger passed out some-where in my apartment? I'd never had a one-night stand, but lately the combination of loneliness and romance novels had made me mighty horny. Throw alcohol into the mix and who knew what I was ca-pable of? "What guy?"

"I can't remember his name. Rob? Ron? Rich? You seriously don't remember him?"

Leaning against the wall for support, I eyed the door to my spare bedroom and asked, "You let me take a guy home?" My voice had crept up three octaves.

"I tried to stop you, but you started talking about women's rights and how it was your choice to hoochify, so I left you to it. I mean, who am I to cock block you?"

My body wasn't sore like I'd had sex, but maybe alcohol was dulling the pain. Then again, I hadn't had sex in so long it could have changed. Maybe it no longer caused soreness and heartache. "Please tell me you're joking."

She laughed again. "So totally kidding. You danced a lot, but always by yourself. Whenever anyone got too close, you ignored them and walked away."

"Great. Even while wasted I'm a bitch."

"Not bitchy, cautious. No one can blame you af-ter... well, after."

I snorted and pushed away from the wall. My legs were still a bit wobbly, but Laura's bluff had shocked my system awake. "I can't believe you scared me like that."

"Shouldn't have drank so much. Although, it was

fun to see you relaxed and enjoying yourself for once."

Her voice held far more emotion than I was prepared to deal with. Stepping into the kitchen, I set the coffeepot to brew and then headed back toward the bathroom. "I hate to cut this call short, but I gotta get ready for work."

"And I have a date with a makeup artist and last-minute changes to discuss with the photographer. I'll see you at the shower."

Inwardly groaning at the reminder, I said goodbye, set my phone on the bathroom counter, and turned on the shower. After I was clean and dressed, I filled up my giant coffee mug and headed downstairs. Then, since coffee is life, I set the downstairs pot to brew and opened up the shop.

My shop.

I'd fallen in love with One More Chapter, the little downtown bookstore, when I was still married. Desperate to revive some sort of physical relationship with my mostly absent husband, I'd turned to romance novels for ideas. But, since Wesley was too busy dipping his stick into everyone else's honey pot, my research didn't do shit to spice up our love life. However, I did manage to rekindle my love for reading. While his workdays lengthened (or he got comfortable spending more time with the sluts he was banging), I dove deeper into romantic fantasies about alpha-males who worshiped their women and took care of all their sexual needs, wondering how much spinach or protein drinks or beer or whatever I'd have to feed Wesley before he became one.

Since I preferred paperbacks to eBooks, the

search for book three in a particularly spicy series led me to One More Chapter. Here, nobody knew me. The sweet, elderly owner greeted me and led me to the romance section like I was anybody else. Behind the safety of the barred windows, walking between packed shelves of books, reading in comfy, overstuffed chairs, I didn't have to plot or plan or pit or control.

Here, I could breathe.

But all good things must come to an end, and my little sanctuary was no exception. The sweet, elderly owner decided it was time to retire shortly after Wesley and I had called it quits. I couldn't allow some greedy investor to liquidate the bookstore and turn the space into another hipster coffee joint or cannabis shop. Not when I had the means to save it. So, I swooped in and took over the building lease, bought the business, rented the apartment above it, and began expanding my vast literature empire.

Sure, the business lost money every month, but the smart investments I'd made from my trust fund carried the loss. If there was one thing I've learned over the past three years, it was that peace and love were worth far more than any amount of money. This place was my peace and my love now, and I'd give every penny I owned to keep it alive. Just breathing in the book smells and walking down the crowded aisles soothed my raging migraine. I perched on the stool behind the counter, found my place in my latest romance story, and drifted off into the fantasy land only a good book could provide.

About a half hour, three chapters, and two cups of coffee later, the bell above the front door chimed.

Pleasantly surprised, I set my book down and looked up, preparing to greet my first customer of the day. At the sight of who had come in, the greeting froze on my lips. Standing close to six-and-a-half feet tall and wearing the same inviting smirk that seemed to grace all his pictures, Marcus "Havoc" Wilson filled the doorway. And I mean, he *filled* the doorway. Everything about him was big, muscular, and imposing, blocking out the sunlight and dampening the sounds of the city.

He was like a shield, blocking me from the world.

After the hours I'd spent scanning the web for juicy details on the Kinlan scandal, I'd recognize the biker anywhere. I just never expected to see him in person. Wearing faded blue jeans, dirty work boots, and a leather biker vest over a tight black T-shirt, he was one hundred percent, grade A, pure male, exuding sex and power like rays of sunshine penetrating my cold, dead love life. His testosterone levels had to be off the charts. They tempted me to close my eyes and bask in his manliness. Instead, I drank in his appearance once again, pausing to appreciate the size of his massive hands and feet.

No doubt this man was enormous everywhere. The thought stirred something to life inside me and heated my entire store.

"Mornin'," he said, closing the door behind him. Such a deep, sexy voice. Deep and sexy enough to send vibrations straight to my lady parts. If that sound was coming through a speaker, I'd be tempted to sit on said speaker and work some stuff out.

I needed to get a grip.

Actually, I needed to get laid. And to stop reading romance novels. And to stop drinking. What if he wasn't real, but just some figment of my imagination spawned from loneliness, desperation, and booze?

"You're open, right?" he asked.

He sure sounded real

"The sign says you're open. I can come back later if you're not." He reached for the doorknob.

The idea of him leaving spurred me to action, freeing me from whatever spell his unexpected presence put me under. I stepped forward, ready to tackle him if he tried to escape. "Sorry. Yes. I'm open."

He cocked an eyebrow.

Unintentional sexual innuendo for the win. Heat flooded my cheeks. "The store's open, I mean. You're... you're Marcus Wilson, aren't you?"

His eyebrow dropped, and his expression darkened. "Havoc. Please. Do I know you?"

"Did Laura put you up to this?" Had my sister really contacted him and sent him my direction? I'd kill her. Or I'd hug her. I was so confused I didn't know what I'd do.

"Laura?" He tilted his head to the side staring at me like I was a puzzle. Either he was an excellent actor, or he had no clue who I was talking about. Carefully watching me, he shook his head. "Sorry. I don't know any Laura. I'm just here looking for a book."

Could it be true? Had the universe brought him to my doorstep out of mere coincidence? If so, I'd just made a complete fool of myself. "Right. A book. I can help you with that." Scooting down the counter to my computer, I pretended we hadn't just shared an award-winning awkward moment and got down to business. "Do you know the title, author, or genre?"

He stared at me, no doubt trying to determine my level of sanity and possibly marveling at my recovery skills before answering, "Something about keeping flowers alive."

Come on. This had to be some sort of setup. No way was a man like Havoc searching for a book about flowers. I wanted to laugh and tell him I was on to his and Laura's little game, but his expression remained serious, making me second guess myself. Fingers hovering over my keyboard, I considered the circumstances that would send him after a book about flowers. Maybe it was a gift? For whom? He wasn't wearing a wedding ring, so I went fishing.

"Who's the gardener?" I asked. "You or your significant other?" It was a blatant, shameless line, but I'd cast it, and there was no reeling it in now. At least not until I saw whether he'd bite.

He watched me, his expression curious and a little amused. "No significant other. Just me."

Okay. Apparently big, buff motorcycle men who beat up rapists *did* garden. Who knew? I started a digital search through my inventory while a voice in the back of my mind kept pointing out that he was single. Not only had he shown up in my bookstore, but he was unattached. And, he would make a perfect date for the wedding. The old me would have manipulated him into being my plus one, but after being ostracized, my confidence in that particular skill was shaky at best. I needed the perfect bait to snag this local hero. Since I no longer had power or influence, I had to figure out something else of value to offer him in exchange for his help.

"What sort of flowers are you trying to grow?" I asked.

"A variety. Here, let me show you some pictures. That might help." He whipped out his phone and swiped through images of a flower box, pointing as he called out their names. "These are daisies. Those are daffodils. I can't remember what that one's called. There's a tulip. I transplanted them about a week ago. They did well for a couple of days, and then they all up and died on me. A friend suggested I find a book that'll tell me what I did wrong and how to keep the next batch alive."

He was telling the truth. Holy crap. Marcus "Havoc" Wilson, the man, the myth, the legend who'd brought Mayor Kinlan to justice, was trying his hand at gardening and had come to me for help. Right when *I* needed help. An idea formed in my mind.

"Come with me," I said, putting a little extra sway in my hips as I circled the counter and headed toward the non-fiction section of the shop. Scanning the gardening books, I selected the thickest, most dreadfully overwhelming books I could find and stacked them on top of the shelf. When I finished, the stack was six high and made Justine's pre-med textbooks look like easy reading. "I suggest you start with these."

His eyes widened. He picked up the top book

and thumbed through pages. "Don't you have an abridged version, or an easy start guide or something?"

Yes, I did, and no, I would not be offering it to him. It was a dirty trick, but I was desperate. I needed his help, and this was all I could think of.

"Not a big reader, I take it?"

"I read just fine, but I prefer stories that interest me. Call me crazy, but I don't think a..." he flipped to the last page, "six hundred- and thirty-six-page book on gardening will be very interesting."

Big pages, too. Lots of writing. It would be a snooze fest for even the most ravenous of floraphiles. "Maybe we can work something else out?" I plucked the book from his hands, closed it, and returned it to the pile.

"What do you have in mind?" he asked, cocking his head to the side.

He was so big. Scary big. Could I trust him? The on-line news articles labeled Havoc and Dead Presidents Motorcycle Club as 'Helpers of the City.' But what if they were wrong? What if he was dangerous? Then again, could he possibly be more dangerous than me?

Swallowing back my fear and anxiety, I replied, "A deal. An exchange."

He continued to watch me. "I'm listening."

"My parents have an excellent gardener. One of the best in Seattle. He owes me a favor, and I could arrange for him to take a look at your flower bed and let you know what's going on and how to fix it."

He nodded. "And in return...?"

How could I ask a perfect stranger to accompany

me to an event as important as my sister's wedding without sounding like a desperate loser? If only there was a book on that. "I need a date."

His eyebrows rose in surprise as his gaze raked over my body, and there was no mistaking his interest. Score. "You're asking me out?"

"Yes. To my sister's wedding."

"To a wedding?" He rubbed the back of his neck. "Shit. You don't fuck around. Look, miss..."

"Julia. Julia Edwards."

"Julia." He rolled my name around on his tongue like a decadent treat he was tasting for the first time. "You're an attractive woman. I'm sure you'd have no trouble finding a date and you don't know shit about me. Let me give you the first lesson; I'm not stupid." He checked out the shelf and selected a small, no-nonsense guide for gardening. "I know how to find a book. I'm also familiar with the internet. The only reason I stopped in was because you're on my way home and I try to support local businesses. What I don't understand is why you're trying to play me like I don't know my ass from a hole in the ground. What's really going on with this wedding?"

More lies flooded my mind. I could have employed flattery, flirted for all I was worth, or bribed him to do it, but I was rusty, and Havoc had already seen through my bullshit. He was a down-to-earth good guy, and he deserved an honest answer. "Because, you're a helper of Seattle and I need help. I need... protection."

4

Havoc

I COULDN'T SEEM to wrap my mind around what the fuck was going on. The hot, curvy red-head with porcelain skin and big green eyes had been checking me out and flirting with me since I'd walked into her bookstore. Not that I minded her attention. Not in the least. In fact, the way her eyes darkened every time her gaze went to my chest and arms was downright ego boosting. She walked past me, and a sweet, soft scent caught my attention. The broad smelled incredible.

While following her to the correct section of the bookstore, I got an eyeful of her round, juicy ass. She had one of those natural, perfect hourglass fig-ures, heavy on the top, heavy on the bottom, shapely legs that were no stranger to the gym. Just thinking about the things I could do to that body was making my pants uncomfortable. I adjusted myself and tried to pay attention to the big ass books she kept piling on top of the bookshelf.

I knew she was up to something, but damn, I had not been prepared for what she wanted from me. Don't get me wrong, I wasn't opposed to dating her—hell, I'd be all over that—but to a wedding? What kind of broad tried to trick a perfect stranger into going to a wedding with her? The crazy kind. I took a step back, knowing I should get the fuck out of there, but her eyes... those goddamn green headlamps glowed with so much pain and desperation I was having a hard time walking away from her.

"I need... protection," she said, sounding desperate and scared.

Those were the magic words. They made the hair on the back of my neck stand up and my feet stick to the ground. I couldn't go anywhere until I found out what was happening and made sure she was safe. Link has called me a sucker for a sob story, and goddammit, I know he's right. Especially when that sob story came with a nice rack and a round ass.

"Is someone trying to hurt you?" I asked. I didn't put up with men roughing up women. Never have, never would. If some asshole thinks he's big enough to slap around a girl, he should be big enough to take me on. And I'd be more than happy to let him try.

"Not physically." She took a deep breath, and her big tits bounced as she let it out. "My little sister's getting married and my ex will be there with his flavor of the week."

Sounded like drama, and I tried to keep that shit out of my life. Still, she was sexy as fuck and flashing me all good signs, and everyone knew weddings made bitches horny. Yes, my mind went there as my

46

gaze drifted back down to her tits. What could I say? I'm a man, and she had the type of body that made smart men do stupid shit.

Also, she'd asked for my help. Not like I thought I was some sort of hero. No, my problem was the opposite. I'd destroyed so much in my life that helping people gave me the chance to balance the scales a little. A shot to make right on somebody else's wrongs. So, I felt out the situation to decide if I could handle her level of crazy. "Your ex is going to your sister's wedding?"

"Our parents are good friends and business partners. They're extremely successful and wealthy. They don't let little things like the comfort or happiness of their children stand in the way of business dealings and public impressions."

"That's fucked up."

"Power comes with an expensive price tag. You must bid high and be willing to sell everything to make the payment. That's what makes it so appealing." The smile she shot me was self-deprecating, and I could tell the shit she was spewing had been spoon-fed to her since birth. Her demons were strong, and they'd been with her for most of her life. But she was smart, and a fighter. I could help a smart fighter.

"And you're afraid of your ex?" I asked.

"No. Oh, hell no." She chortled. "I'm afraid of me. Of what I might do if I see that pencil-dicked bastard again. I don't need your protection from Wesley. You need to protect *him* from *me*. No, it's more than that. I need you to contain me. To keep me from reverting to my old self."

This was getting interesting. "What do you mean?"

"Wesley is weak. Stupid." Her face twisted in disgust. "I could ruin him. I could ruin most of them if they pushed me too far. But I don't want to be that person anymore. I need someone with me who's big, strong, and smart enough to keep the power-hungry bitch inside of me and off the playground. You used to be Special Forces, right? That means you're smart and strong." I eyed him up and down. "And you're obviously big."

"Yet you tried to pull that shit with the books on me."

"And you called me on it," she said. "Which means I won't be able to manipulate you. I need that. I'm trying really hard to be a decent human being and leave my past behind me, but this wedding will threaten my resolve."

"Where and when is the wedding?"

"This coming Saturday at three p.m. at the Shoreline Country Club on Bainbridge Island."

Ritzy place. Julia wasn't playing when she said her parents were loaded.

"I know it's short notice and I'm sorry." She winced. "It's a suit and tie event, so no bikes. But we could take my Mercedes."

Her assumption that I only had a bike rubbed me wrong. Sure, I wouldn't be hosting any parties on Bainbridge Island, but I did all right for myself. I had a house and a yard to keep up. Couldn't exactly put lumber and a lawn mower on the back of my Fatboy. And even if I didn't have some sort of cage, I'd rent one. No way in hell I'd let her drive me to a wedding of rich white people. Be the black man in the passenger's seat? Fuck that.

I should walk.

I should get the fuck out of that bookstore and never look back.

But the fear and desperation in Julia's eyes held me hostage. I could help her. As crazy as she sounded, I understood her. I too had a beast inside of me, and he was a motherfucker to contain. Last time he'd gotten free, I'd put Noah Kinlan in the hospital. I could have just ripped his scrawny ass off of that girl and called the cops, but the beast needed more. It needed the sound of Noah's bones breaking and the scent of his blood. I probably would have killed Noah if the guys from the bar hadn't shown up. Yeah, I understood Julia's predicament all too well, and I needed her to know I wasn't the hero she was looking for.

"No matter what you read about me, I'm no saint, Julia."

She took a step closer, invading my space with her floral-scented tempting body. She knew what she was doing, how she was affecting me. I could see it in the smile that ghosted her lips and the shift in her stance. The way she stuck her tits out to tease me. "Good. A saint wouldn't survive two seconds in my world. I need a devil who's figured out how to lock himself away."

She was tempting me, inviting my beast to come play, testing me to see if my resolve was strong enough to contain him. She was showing me she understood my struggle and saw who I really was. Helping her would be a gamble. Get us together, and we could either save the world or destroy it.

I never could turn down a challenge. But I wasn't careless and needed to make sure she was committed to the cause before I agreed. "I have three conditions."

"You'll do it?" she asked, her eyes wide as she grabbed my arm. "You'll be my date for the wedding?"

I nodded. "As long as you agree to the conditions."

She eyed me, making it clear she wasn't used to resistance. "Okay...?"

"I'm driving. I'll pick you up."

"Great. Not a problem. What's the second one?"

"No more lies. I won't put up with you trying to play me. No games. At the first hint of that bullshit, I'll bounce. I can't help you unless you're straight up with me. Nothing but honesty from here on out."

She filled her cheeks with air and then slowly blew it out. "That's a toughie. It's like second-nature for me to push and pull and—"

"I'm on your side, Julia. I'm trying to help you and I won't put up with that shit."

Her gaze raked over me again, and her eyes darkened. She liked that. It turned her on that she couldn't push me around. I filed that little tidbit away for later.

"Okay." She took another deep breath. "Nothing but honesty from here on out."

"Third, if I do this, not only will you hook me up with this gardener, but you'll also help me out with something next Saturday. My club is hosting a dinner for the homeless and—"

"You want a donation? Sure. Absolutely. How much?"

"I don't want a donation," I said with a chuckle, amused at how quickly her mind went to money. She'd definitely been raised rolling in it. "I want you to come and serve food to the homeless."

Her jaw dropped. "You want *me* to serve food to the homeless? After everything I just told you? Have you been listening? I'm dangerous, Havoc."

"Only to the people who can offer you something. You're like an addict, babe."

She stared at me for a beat and I could almost see the wheels in her head spinning, trying to follow my thought process. "I think you're oversimplifying my condition."

I shook my head. "You're complicating it."

She folded her arms. "Okay, I'll bite. How am I like an addict?"

"You did something you regret, and you want to get out of that lifestyle. But now you have to attend this party where you'll be tempted to use again. You're afraid you won't be able to withstand the temptation, so you're calling in the big guns."

Her gaze went directly to my arms. "You do have big guns." She let the rest of what I'd said sink in for a few moments, then sucked in a breath and took a step back. "Shit. Okay, I am like an addict."

"And when addicts want to change their behavior, we have to get them out of their own mind. Get them to step away from their own problems. We encourage them to serve. To do something for someone else. So, that's my third condition."

"And you'll be there?" she asked. "You'll keep me from freaking out on anyone?"

"Yeah. I'll have your back. There and at the wedding."

She threw her hands in the air. "Why not? Sure. I'll come and serve homeless people next Saturday, I'll try this whole honesty thing with you, and you can drive. Now, you'll need a suit. If you follow me to the front, I'll get you some cash to cover the expense."

After all the progress we'd made, that felt like a slap in the face. "What the fuck?" I asked.

She paused mid-turn. "What?"

"What about me makes you so sure I don't own a suit? You think I need your money, Julia? That I can't buy my own suit?"

Confusion crossed her face, and then her expression softened. "No. That's not what I meant. Your financial status is none of my business. You're doing me a huge favor, and it would be rude if I didn't at least offer to pay your expenses."

Her explanation softened the blow a little, but it still rankled.

"I'm a man, babe. I'll buy my own goddamn suit."

I expected her to be scared or upset like most women were when they got a glimpse of my temper, but Julia's eyes lit up with something else entirely. Excitement? Arousal? She liked it—liked me—of that, I was certain. Biting her lip, she nodded in agreement. "Of course. I see that now."

Her voice was deeper. Huskier. Yep, she was turned on. Maybe I'd get a little something out of helping her after all. Before I could think too much about that, my phone buzzed. I tugged it from my pocket and saw I was being dispatched to an accident site. As one of three tow truck drivers for Formation Auto Repair (the shop owned and run by the Dead Presidents MC) I was on call today. Lousy timing, since I'd really like to spend more time trying to figure Julia out.

"I gotta run. Work calls."

Her eyes hardened as she watched my phone slide back into my pocket. Did she think I was blowing her off? There had to be history there. Hot as she was, she sure came with a shit-ton of baggage. But as my gaze drifted over her fan-fucking-tastic figure once again, I decided she might be worth the trouble.

"Hand me your phone and I'll put my number in it," I said.

Without hesitation, she passed her cell to me. I sent myself a text and handed it back.

I needed to jet, but there was something else I had to know. "Your family... they're not racist, are they?"

Her brow furrowed. "I don't think so. It's not very becoming to be racist these days, and the Edwards always keep up with the latest trends. Besides, we have a wealthy African-American family on the guest list."

The country club's token black family. Bet I'd fit right in.

"Thank you again for doing this," she said.

That heat was back in her eyes, making me want to explore the depths of her gratitude, but I had a crash to get to. "Yeah. No problem. Don't forget to send me the information for the gardener."

She picked up her phone and started typing. "Doing it right now. His name's Javier. I'll call ahead and tell him to expect your call."

I took a step toward the door. "What time should I pick you up Saturday?"

"The ferry leaves at one-ten, so... noonish?"

"All right. See you Saturday."

She said goodbye, and I headed out. I had a car to tow and a suit to buy, and before I even climbed into the tow truck, Julia had texted me the phone number to her parents' gardener. I had no clue what the fuck I'd just signed up for, but it promised to be interesting.

5

Havoc

THE CRASH I'D been routed to was on I5 southbound, just north of Exit 165A—the James Street exit—one of the busiest stretches of freeway in the whole damn city. By the time I arrived, traffic was already backing up and police were doing their damnedest to route rubber necking, nosy-ass drivers around the accident. One of Seattle's finest broke away from the group and waved me forward, directing me toward the shoulder. Apparently, it would be a while before I could hook up. Dammit. The bastards had interrupted my time with Julia, so I could sit out here and wait. Such bullshit. But since I hadn't had the best luck with cops—especially not lately—and the club needed this contract with the city, I kept my attitude in check. Head down, I parked where I was told to, rolled down my window, and waited for them to get their shit together.

The two ambulances parked in front of the cop

cars were blocking my view of the scene. Curious about how far along they were, I leaned over my seat to get a look and saw two cars. One was sandwiched between the guardrail and the other car, looking like a goddamn accordion. Rescue workers shouted to each other while a woman wailed about someone named Jimmy. That was far more than I needed to see or hear. Memories tugged at the back of my mind. Refusing to give in to them, I righted myself and watched the traffic, trying to block out the woman's desperate cries.

I shouldn't be here for this shit. They weren't supposed to call until they were ready for me. Some new asswipe must have been eager to get the wreck cleaned up so traffic could flow again and made the call too damn early.

A fire truck arrived, parking beside the ambulances. Firemen piled out, carrying the jaws of life toward the scene. Minutes later, metal screeched, adding its own noise to the chaos. A news helicopter swooped in, dipping low so the camera crew could get their shot of the scene.

Too many sounds and sights. The familiarity of it tugged at my subconscious, threatening to pull me under. I fought to stay in the present, but my goddamn memories wouldn't let up. Heart and mind racing, my mind transported me back to Kobani, Syria.

Link jogged in front of me, his expression pinched tight as he signaled for the team to enter the border town. It was my first mission as an Army Special Forces Weapons Specialist. We were going in on the tail of a US-led air strike that had targeted Islamist militants, and our mission was to take out some lead ISIS bastard who'd somehow survived. This air strike had been the last of more than one hundred and thirty strikes in the area, sending over five hundred ISIS Al-Nasra Front shitheads to hell where they belonged.

We were the good guys, and we specialized in ridding the world of the dangerous motherfuckers who wanted to blow it to shit. What we did was important. Necessary. I'd been thirteen when the Twin Towers crumbled, and I'd never forget the fear and anger I felt at the bastards who crashed those planes into the towers. My mom and sisters huddled in front of the television, holding each other and crying as we watched the explosions again and again. People jumping out of the goddamn buildings to get away from the smoke. That's something you can't un-see. I knew right then that I was going to enlist, because I wanted to make sure nobody ever attacked the US again. I trained, I fought, I prepared, and I felt damn lucky to be part of a team of soldiers who felt the same way.

But I hadn't expected the civilian casualties.

Innocent people died in wars. Shit happened. Not every bullet found its mark. Sometimes bombs took out the wrong people. I knew the risks. But knowing was not the same as seeing it. Not in the least.

We entered the city on foot, at dusk, under the cover of smoke still lingering from the air strikes. Climbing over rubble, we skirted the more populated streets and hurried toward our mark. The cowardly motherfucker was holed up in an underground children's refuge, and getting him out of there would be tricky.

As we passed bodies, demolished buildings, running through the wrecked and ravaged city, I reminded my-

self that all this destruction was necessary. Couldn't be helped. We had to stop the bad guys. I knew the truth of that in the very essence of my being. If we didn't attack them, they'd come for us. Some other American landmark would serve as the target, and we could not allow that to happen.

Rounding the corner of a partially leveled building, we came across a child. He couldn't have been more than four or five, and was sitting beside the body of a woman, just staring at her. Blank look on his face, no tears or anything. His gaze shifted, and he made eye contact with me. The kid looked hollow. Empty. Shit, it was crazy. I swear I'll never forget that look in his eyes as long as I live.

We were the good guys, and we'd killed his mom, no doubt leaving him an orphan. The air strikes were neces- sary. Her death had been unintentional. This kind of shit happened in wars. None of that knowledge stopped me from smelling the coppery-sweet scent of his mom's blood mixed with the stench of shit.

And God help me, as I stared at the kid with the hollow eyes, I wondered if he'd grow up to be a fucking militant. Would he hide the IEDs that took out my con- voy? Would he raid our camps and steal our shit? Would I have to put a bullet between his eyes?

Dark, fucked up thoughts. They made me feel like a monster. He was just a kid. But as we passed him, I kept my M16 ready, and didn't take my eyes off him.

Someone shouted.

Sounding an alarm? We couldn't allow that. Turning to find him and fire, my world blurred, bringing me back to the present.

I was sitting in my tow truck, my hands outstretched like I was holding my M16. The ambulances were gone, and a cop stood beside my tow truck, watching me like I was high on something.

I'd let the past drag me back again.

Disgusted with myself and angry that I was still so fucking helpless to control my triggers, I took a deep breath and dropped my hands. My heart continued to race, and the sound of gunfire lingered. No, wait. That was the news helicopter.

Fucking chopper. It didn't even sound like gunfire.

Sometimes it felt like I was losing my ever-loving mind.

I made eye contact with the cop, silently reassuring him I was clean and sober. He watched me for a beat, and then waved me forward and directed me toward the wreck. Another officer pointed me to the second car, an Audi. Since the front end was smashed into a Camry, I backed up to its ass end, hooked it up, and got the hell out of there.

6

Julia

HAVOC SAID HE would be my date for the wedding, and I had no reason to doubt him, but I still worried he'd come to his senses and change his mind. I mean, I hadn't exactly come off as sane. I paced back and forth through the front of my bookstore, scrolling through the text messages we'd sent back and forth since. His first text was a thank you for sending the gardener to help him. Javiar had gone out Monday and figured out the problem—some PH imbalance in the soil paired with over watering—and Havoc planted new flowers that were now thriving. He was so proud, he sent me pictures.

There was something sweet and unexpected about a man who looked like Havoc sending me pictures of his flowers. Clearly a man who did things like that wouldn't just up and ditch a woman who was counting on him. At least that's what I kept telling myself.

After his flower fiasco was taken care of, Havoc continued to text me. I'd get a "Hi," here, and a "How are you doing?" there. Nothing too heavy, just friendly texts that provided quick escapes from all the time I spent dreading Laura's wedding. Havoc asked what I was wearing to the wedding, so I sent him a picture. He sent back a drooling emoji that made me laugh and stole away some of the anxiety I had about wearing such a revealing gown. I asked about his suit and he sent me a picture. I upped his emoji game by sending two drool faces and a winky face. All our correspondence was light, friendly, and flirty, and I couldn't find anything that should have scared him off.

Maybe two drool emojis and a winky face had been too much?

"You look gorgeous," Justine said, glancing up from her textbook long enough to flash me a reassuring smile.

"You really do, dear," a sweet elderly lady perusing the romance section added. "Might want to grab a sweater or something, though. Not much fabric to that dress."

I cringed, knowing she was right. My sister's bridesmaids were all little whores, and they'd outvoted me, choosing bridesmaid's gowns that were gorgeous, but revealing. Really revealing. Lavender, beaded, and sleeveless, the unique halter style dress had a keyhole front that started three inches below my collarbone and ran down to the bottom of my breastbone. The back was open to right above my ass, with a few thin straps of fabric crisscrossing to keep it from falling off every time I leaned forward.

The only real coverage was between my waist and the floor. At least my feet would stay warm in their strappy white heels.

The design forced me to abandon my normal strapless bra for a pair of adhesive silicone lift D cups. Laura's little brideswhores all had perfect bodies and fake boobs, so they didn't have to worry about things like keeping their partially exposed breasts in place or their back fat from showing.

Bitches.

I'd been dieting and working out every day since we'd ordered the dresses, and was pleased to admit that I looked damn good. The gown embellished my curves and made me feel glamorous. Sexy. I couldn't remember the last time I felt that way.

With my long hair styled in a fancy updo with soft ringlets framing my face (courtesy of the salon down the street) and my makeup flawless (courtesy of my contouring wizardry skills), I was ready to face down the country club of people I wanted to incinerate. All I needed was my date.

As if summoned by my mounting fear that he wouldn't show, a newer model blue Toyota Tundra with a king cab pulled up in front of the bookstore. Even though I couldn't see the driver from where I stood, I knew it would be Havoc. The truck looked like it was custom-built for him: big, masculine, and powerful. The door opened, closed, and then he stood on the sidewalk wearing a suit.

My breath hitched.

I'd grown up around men in suits, and after everything I went through, men in suits looked like pompous assholes to me. But not Havoc. Havoc looked delicious. His suit was top-notch. No department store threads for this sexy biker. The lines were clean, the fabric was thick and high quality, and it fit like a glove. It had to be custom tailored. No way did stores stock his size, so either he had it hanging in his closet, or he forked over some serious dough to get it done so quickly. And this sexy biker was taking me—a screwed up woman whom he didn't even know—to a wedding full of complete strangers where he'd stick out like a sore thumb.

He really was a good guy. His selflessness made my eyeballs burn.

Blinking back tears, I called out, "He's here!" to Justine and opened the door.

"You kids have fun," she replied. "Make good choices."

It was something I said whenever her boyfriend picked her up, and it made me smile. Especially since Havoc had frozen and was staring at me with ravenous eyes that made me want to make bad choices. The funnest kind of horrible choices.

We stared at each other for a couple of seconds, his gaze roaming up and down my body appreciatively as mine did the same. The lines of the suit highlighted his broad shoulders, muscular arms, and incredible legs. It made him seem bigger, more threatening, larger than life.

So hot.

"Damn," he said, finally. Approaching, he circled me, his heated gaze burning through my dress and warming me in a way no sweater could. "*This* is what you're wearing to the wedding?"

I smiled at him over my shoulder. "I sent you a picture."

He rubbed a hand across the back of his neck, meeting my gaze. "Sure as hell didn't look like this on the hanger. Your ass is definitely gonna need protection."

My smile widened. "That's why you're here, right?" Although we both knew it was the country club that needed protection.

He swallowed and let his gaze drift back down my body. "Yeah, but who's gonna protect you from me?"

The dark, lust-filled look in his eyes made my pulse race and my knees weaken. I'd never felt more desirable in my life. If I said the word, Havoc would no doubt take me up to my apartment and ravage me. And oh my god, I could use a good ravaging.

But our presence was required at the impending wedding of awkwardness, so any ravaging would have to wait.

"We should get going," I breathed, making myself step toward the truck.

Havoc nodded and hurried to open the door. "Here, let me help you," he said, holding out his arm. "I haven't got the nerf bars mounted yet, and that dress looks hella tight. Wouldn't want you to rip it."

His expression said differently, making me feel like my dress was in danger of getting shredded, but not accidentally. And if he kept looking at me like that, I'd probably let him have at it. Hell, I'd welcome it. Averting my eyes to tamp down on the temptation, I asked, "Nerf bars?"

"Side steps."

Looking down, I saw what he was talking about. With nothing between the ground and the bottom of the truck, I'd have to hike my leg up almost to my knee to get in. Which was saying a lot, because I stood close to five-foot-ten without the three-inch strappy heels I currently had on. Wondering how I was going to manage this in a tight dress—even with the help of Havoc's arm—I looked from him to the truck, and then back to him. He cracked a smile, grabbed me around the waist, and hoisted me up like I weighed nothing at all.

When he released me, one of his warm, giant hands brushed against the bare skin of my back, sending goosebumps over my entire body. His gaze locked with mine and he leaned in until our faces were inches away before drifting down to the slit between my breasts. Havoc was obviously a boob man. Good to know. He sucked in a deep breath and bent to tuck the train of my dress safely inside the cab. He closed my door and circled around to the driver's side.

My chest heaved as I sucked in air, trying to calm my racing heart. The guy was too intense, too sexual, too much. Last time we'd been together he'd been chastising me for trying to play him and calling me a druggie. But now he was like a walking, breathing, buff, hot platter of sex, and I was cold and starving. Wondering how I'd survive the fifteen-minute drive, not to mention the thirty-five-minute ferry ride, without devouring him, I kept my gaze locked straight ahead and tried not to notice the way his arms flexed as he got behind the wheel.

I failed.

He turned over the ignition, and the truck came to life with a manly roar. I tried to picture Wesley driving a vehicle like this but couldn't. It was too virile. It'd make him look tiny, and he'd feel emasculated, which was why he drove sports cars that made women ignore his micro penis.

"You should brief me on what to expect," Havoc said, merging into traffic. "Other than a bunch of rich white people and a token black family."

"Entitled, rich white people," I corrected. "But don't worry, it won't all be stories of hunting and golf. My great aunt, Martha, will provide inappropriate entertainment by getting plastered and feeling up the waiters."

"One in every family. Can't anyone keep the booze away from her?"

"They try." A guilty smile tugged at my lips. "But Laura and I sneak her drinks. We figure she's old and if she wants to get drunk and hit on the young'ns, who are we to stop her?"

He chuckled, shaking his head. "And the rest of your family?"

"Dad's a workaholic. Mom is a social dictator who makes or breaks people's societal standings through her pull with all the local charity events. I only have one grandma left, and she's basically an older, more bitter version of Mom. Two of my uncles will be there, talking shop or boring anyone stupid enough to listen to their harrowing tales of murdering defenseless animals or small white balls. My aunts will express their disappointment in my purchase of a bookstore when such things are outdated and disappearing while stabbing me with advice about how to snag another husband. My cousins... who knows? We're not close anymore on account of them being perfect and me being tainted."

And that was a lot of family drama to vomit at him. I wouldn't be surprised if Havoc dropped me off at the ferry and drove away.

"Tainted?" he asked, arching a brow.

"Divorced. That's how my family views it."

He gaped at me. "You mean to tell me nobody in your family is divorced?"

"I'm the first. A real trailblazer. My parents are super proud."

"How the fuck is that even possible? No one in my family is still with their first spouse. Not even my two married sisters."

Folding my hands in my lap, I tried to think of the best way to describe our twisted take on wedding vows. "Marriage in our family is a business transaction. If you're not getting enough sex or love or whatever you need at home, you can find it on the side. Just be discreet, and nobody will judge you for it. Especially since they're all sleeping around. But marriage is a contract, and we don't break contracts."

"So, it's okay to cheat, but not to divorce?"

I shrugged. "I don't make the rules; I just break them."

"Is that what happened between you and the ex?" Havoc asked. "Did he cheat?"

I snorted. "It's complicated."

"You said I was smart. I might understand."

He was smart, and the way he followed along seeming genuinely interested was impressive. "Wesley's father is my dad's business partner. Our marriage made sense on a lot of levels. My mother has been training me for a long time to do what she does, and—"

"The social dictator gig?" he asked.

"Yes. And my marriage to Wesley strengthened both of our families and the business. We joined the game, created alliances, and cut down enemies. We were virtually untouchable."

"What happened?"

"Several of my old friends got jealous and teamed up to take us down. But not with well-placed rumors, back-handed compliments, or stolen investment leads like civilized people. They went for the weak link in our relationship. Wesley. And his ego is so enormous that he believed they all wanted to fuck him. After they were done, they convinced him that Laura wanted his body as well."

"Your sister?"

"The one and only."

"You're shittin' me?"

"Nope. It's the absolute truth. He propositioned her, and she turned him down and called me to break the news. He must have found someone else to dip into that night, because he was late coming home. When he finally arrived, I was waiting with the hunting rifle Dad had bought him for a wedding present."

Havoc pulled into the parking lot for the ferry, parked, and then turned his full attention onto me.

"I tried to kill him, but the chickenshit hit the ground. I'd never shot a rifle before and wasn't expecting the kick, but I still clipped him in the ass. Holy crap, my shoulder was sore for days. Pretty much annihilated our front door, which was convenient, since the last of my bags were packed and at my feet. I picked them up, walked over his bleeding ass, got in my car, and left."

Havoc stared at me in open-mouthed awe, and I got the feeling I should have left out this story time detail until he was captive on the ferry and couldn't bail on me. "You shot him?"

"Look, I'm trying really hard to be honest with you, so I need you not to give me the judgy eyes. It was a flesh wound. He lived, unfortunately. Trust me, he needed it to toughen him up a bit. Also, you must understand that I was faithful from the beginning. I knew from the time we were kids that I was going to marry him, and my mom convinced me that nobody else would be good enough for me. My family groomed me for Wesley. I dated no one else, never kissed anyone else, never..." My throat tightened. I swallowed and gave myself a moment before continuing, "He promised me that our marriage would be different. That it would mean something more than a solid business deal. I made a vow to him, and I stayed true. Not only did that asshole break his vow, but he still doesn't even realize that those bitches played him. And my own parents played me! They made him out to be this perfect catch, but he was the fish I should have gutted and then thrown back into the pond. If my shoulder hadn't been so damn sore from the kickback of the first shot, I would have tried again."

Havoc was still staring at me, making my stomach clench in fear that I'd scared him off. I opened my mouth to continue my defense, but he held up a hand.

"I get it. You had a partner you planned to take over the world with. Then your partner follows a trail of bread crumbs and ends up in a trap while you find out that the world is nothing but a ball of shit wrapped in shiny paper."

The absurdity of it all made me giggle. He really got it. "Yes. Exactly."

"You don't want that world anymore, do you?"

I shook my head. "No. I want my bookstore and my little apartment. I don't want to fight over a shiny ball of shit anymore."

"Good. We're gonna get you through this wedding just fine. Now, since I don't want to beat the shit out of some horny-ass men checking you out in that dress, I need you to stay here while I go get us tickets for the ferry."

"You're coming back, right?" I asked. "Please tell me this isn't the part where you realize this is entirely too much crazy for you, abandon your truck, and head for the hills."

He climbed out of the truck and turned to look at me. "Babe. I'd never abandon my truck." Then he gave me another sexy smirk, closed the door and walked off.

I admired the view that his incredible backside provided until he stepped out of sight. Then I took my first relaxed breath of the day. Possibly of the month. For the first time ever, I'd told someone about my ex without wanting to drive to Wesley's house and set it on fire. The anger and pain were gone. Maybe Havoc was right, and we could get me through this wedding after all.

7

Havoc

"**W**ELL AREN'T YOU a sight for sore eyes?" Julia's great aunt asked, wrapping the bony fingers of one hand around my bicep and giving it a little squeeze. "Oh, that's nice. That's really nice."

Her other hand held a glass of champagne. She tipped it to her lips and took a sip, batting her thin old lady eyelashes at me. We were less than a half hour into the wedding reception and this was the third time she'd approached. When she wasn't blatantly hitting on me, she was canvassing a circle around the table, eyeballing me as she closed in for the kill. I hadn't felt this vulnerable since I was with my team and we were sneaking over the streets of Kobani. This woman was like a drone, powered on Geritol and lust.

"Aunt Martha," Julia said, once again loosening the old lady's hands and extracting her from me.

"Havoc's a guest, and you're making him uncomfortable."

Uncomfortable, my ass. She was making me downright anxious. My head was on a swivel, trying to keep her in sight so she didn't take me by surprise. It wasn't wise to sneak up on a vet. We startled easily, and I didn't want to react and accidentally lay the old woman out. And every time she reached me, she turned into a goddamn octopus, which was why I kept my ass seated as Julia handled her. Last time, I stood —like a gentleman should—only to feel those bony fingers grab my ass. Too far. Appalled, I looked around for witnesses who would call her out for groping me, but the sneaky old bat did it on the down-low so nobody else saw. I sure as hell couldn't draw attention to the situation. Wouldn't put it past these assholes to label me as the problem and call the cops.

"I bet I could make him really comfortable," Aunt Martha said before taking another sip of her champagne. She swayed a little with the effort.

"Aunt Martha!" Julia grabbed her aunt's arm, steadying the old lady.

Aunt Martha's eyes were still raking over my body. "They don't make men like this anymore, sweetheart. When you see one, you gotta grab him and hold on tight." Her free hand made a move to do just that, but Julia angled her away.

"I'll take that into consideration. Here, let me walk you back to your seat." Julia plucked the sloshing glass out of her aunt's hand, draped an arm around her, and half carried her to the end of the table.

When Julia returned, I leaned closer and asked, "Who the fuck is giving her champagne?"

Julia shook her head. "Hard telling. It's a lot more amusing when she's not hitting on my date. Sorry." That had to be her hundredth apology since we'd arrived.

"It's fine," I said, but in truth, nothing was okay. We were sitting at a table with her parents, who'd done their damnedest to ignore me during the meal while trying to bait Julia into giving a fuck about their little society. At least Wesley hadn't approached. Julia had pointed him out to me the minute we walked in and so far, her ex seemed content to glower at us from the corner, surrounded by a bunch of his pussy friends with a skinny brunette on his arm.

"So much has been neglected since you left," her mom said. "Danella has taken over the Thompson Foundation and you know she can't handle it. Not like you could. People aren't donating like they used to, and the events are pitiful."

Julia leaned closer to me until our legs were touching. "I'm sure Danella is doing her best, Mother. She probably needs time to get the hang of things." She leaned against me and whispered, "Poison is illegal, and I would probably regret it. It's a good thing I didn't bring any."

Her mother's eyes narrowed, and she switched tactics. "Well, Jozette's doing a fantastic job with the club house fundraiser. I saw her on Wesley's arm today. It looks like your old friend is trying to completely replace you. Are you going to sit back and allow that, Julia? Because the daughter that I raised—"

"Doesn't exist anymore. I'm sorry, but I have no interest in returning to my club duties. I'm happy where I am." To me, she whispered, "Laxatives won't kill anyone, but they would keep her in the bathroom for a while. Why didn't I think of bringing those?"

Her mother frowned. "I just don't see how running a bookstore could be all that rewarding. Especially not for someone as intelligent as you. I can understand why you don't want to come back, but why don't you do something with your degree? Not something too significant, because you don't want to appear bossy or controlling. But something that showcases your intelligence and makes you more attractive to potential suitors. I know things didn't work out with Wesley, but your father and I have spoken to him and he's willing to—"

I'd had enough. Not only was this bitch ripping apart her daughter's livelihood, but she was disrespecting me by talking about suitors like I wasn't there as Julia's date. How the fuck did she know we weren't serious? Julia had brought me to keep her from freaking out, and I was two seconds from flipping the table and punching Julia's father in the face. He'd been on his phone the entire time, nodding or muttering his agreement whenever his wife requested it. Couldn't he see what this bitch was doing to their daughter? Didn't he care?

I needed to get out of there before I snapped. Pushing back my chair, I stood. "Where's the restroom?"

A look of terror contorted Julia's face as she joined me, straightening her dress before grabbing my hand. "I have to go as well. I'll show you."

Her mom's gaze zeroed in on our intertwined hands and a look of disgust curled her lip before she pasted on her normal mask of neutrality.

I wanted to say something, but Julia tugged me away. As we wove through the tables toward the restrooms, I was met with a mix of scathing looks from the men and interested gazes from the women. On the ferry, Julia had told me that this was the country club the Kinlan's frequented, and as I heard his name whispered, I knew damn well what people were saying about me and didn't care. I could take it. However, I worried about Julia. I squeezed her hand, reassuring her I was still there.

"Thank you," she said, pulling me away from the crowd.

"For what? You don't need my permission or excuses to walk away from them."

"No, but the power still appeals to me. Wesley was weak and got played, but I should have seen it coming. I slipped up. I got cocky and comfortable in my position and the bitches took me down. Mom is challenging me to come back and fix my mistake. To prove I still have what it takes. It's hard to walk away from that."

Probably felt like walking away from a fight while someone was talking shit. "How long has it been since you've been back?"

"A little over a year ago. Since I tried to kill Wesley."

She talked about it like it was nothing. Just an

everyday occurrence. "Did you do any time for that?"

Her brows furrowed. "You mean like jail?"

"Yeah. That's usually where people go for attempted murder." I knew first hand.

A smile ghosted her lips. "Wesley wouldn't turn me in. That would make him look even weaker. And if he tried, our parents wouldn't allow it."

Nothing like rich white privilege. Julia had probably never suffered a consequence in her life until her peers turned on her, but that one time had changed her. It made her turn her back on everything and everyone she knew. It made her want to be a better person.

And that made her even more beautiful.

Her gaze darted to the dance floor, landing on something, or someone, that made her lip curl. Before I could follow her line of sight and figure out what she'd seen, she pointed the opposite direction. "The bathroom's there. I'm going to need a stiffer drink."

She'd already had two glasses of champagne, but they didn't seem to affect her. "You sure that's a good idea?"

"It's a necessity. Want me to order you something?"

A drink sounded like a good idea, but none of that pink shit they were serving. "A beer. Something dark. A stout or a porter."

"You got it. I'll meet you at the bar." As the words left her mouth, she walked past the ladies' room and turned the corner.

After I reemerged from the restroom, I found

Julia sitting at the bar with her sexy back toward me. Damn, I loved that dress, and based on the way every man in the bar was checking her out, I wasn't the only one. Before I could cross the room, Wesley took the stool beside her. Hair gelled, face clean-shaven, hands in the pockets of his suit jacket, he looked every bit the spoon-fed asshole she made him out to be. Her shoulders tensed at his proximity, but she did not back down.

Torn between the need to protect her, and the knowledge that she needed to handle this shit for herself, I got close enough to listen in on their conversation and jump in if she needed me.

"...good together. A power team. What we had was great. It'll take some work, but we can get there again."

"You mean that fantastic relationship where I'm at home playing wife, organizing your schmooze-fests and destroying your enemies while you were sleeping with mine?" Julia asked. "Because that wasn't all that rewarding for me."

"Don't be so dramatic." He pulled a hand out of his pocket to stroke her bare arm with the back of his fingers. "We shared many good times."

She shied away from his touch, leaning closer to the bar to take another drink.

"Yep. My favorite was that time I shot your cheating ass. Heard you needed stitches. That had to hurt. Please tell me it scarred."

The corners of his mouth tightened. "Don't be crude. I managed. And yes, I screwed around, but you always had my heart, Julia."

She snorted. "What heart?"

He spread his hands out, nodding. "Exactly why we're perfect together. None of those messy feelings to impede what's really important."

"That's where you're losing me. We don't value the same things anymore, Wesley. I value loyalty, and you... you value your penis, as pathetic as the little guy is."

He closed the distance between them. "You used to value my penis, too, remember? You didn't think it was too small then."

She placed a hand on his chest and pushed him away. "I was young, naïve, and inexperienced. You told me you were huge, and I believed you. I was faithful, so I had nothing to compare it to. I didn't know what else was out there."

"You still don't."

"Are you so certain?" She took another big gulp.

"I keep tabs on you, Julia. I protect all of my investments."

"Creepy. Perhaps you should focus less on me and more on stringing along your date and pretending you're trying to replace me before she finds someone richer and hotter to bang?"

He glanced over his shoulder to the skinny brunette leaning against the wall like a puppy on a leash. "She knows her place. It's your date I'm worried about." Wesley's gaze cut to me for a second before his attention returned to Julia. "You know he ruined the Kinlans, right?"

"I'm pretty sure the Kinlans ruined themselves when they became underground crime lords."

"He doesn't belong like you do... like *we* do. I know you've fallen from grace, but if you insist on it

79

being over between us, I'm sure I could find you a more suitable catch. Maybe not a club member, but at least a white guy."

Julia straightened and raised her voice. "I don't care what shade his skin is, Havoc is ten times the man you are. Better looking, more intelligent... I bet you haven't even figured out that those sluts played you."

"What?" he asked.

"Forget it. I don't have the time, desire, or crayons to explain it to you. I should have killed you when I had the chance."

A predatory smile stretched across his face as he lowered his voice. I had to strain my ears to hear him. "There you are, my beautiful, terrifying bride. I missed you. You think you have it all figured out, don't you? Bet you never even considered the idea that *I* was the one who orchestrated your fall. But, my lovely, vicious bitch, who do you think told those whores what you were up to in the first place? Once they knew what you were doing, they were all too eager to spread their legs for me. Julia, I fucked every one of your friends, and you had no idea what was going on." He clicked his tongue. "Disappointing. Thought you were smarter than that. But, we all make mistakes and I'm in a forgiving mood, so I'll give you another shot. Come home. We'll get remarried and we can move on from your failure and start over."

"You pompous bitchboy. You want to start over? I wish I'd never fucking met you." Her voice started as a low growl, but grew louder as she added, "I will ruin you. I made you, and I will take your ass down.

I will make sure that everyone knows what a spine-less, pencil-dicked, festering anal scab you are." She scanned her surroundings, likely searching for a weapon.

Shit! Time to move in.

She grabbed her glass. Liquid sloshed as she wound up as if to bash his head in with it. "Fuck that. I'm done with this game. I'll just kill you myself!"

Moving to intercept her, I positioned myself between them and settled my hands on her shoulders. "Julia, look at me."

Her glass was still poised and ready to strike as she tried to get around me. "Let me go, Havoc," she growled. "That crusty twat fucker needs to die."

"You're turning me on, my bride," Wesley said, poking his head around me. "You know I love it when you lose your temper."

"I am not your fucking bride."

Needing her attention, I squeezed her shoulders. "Focus on my voice, babe. Look at me. Don't let him do this to you. You're no longer this person. Don't let him take you there."

Her gaze met mine. She blinked, and a look of total and complete devastation crossed her face as her chest rose and fell. She looked from me to the crowd that was gathering around us, and then back to me. "Dammit. Havoc, I—"

"I know. You're fine. I got you now." I plucked the glass from her hand and set it on the bar. "Let's get you away from him. Dance with me."

"I..." She looked so lost. So unsure of herself. "I got you a beer."

"It's fine. I'm not thirsty anymore. Come on." I took her hand. Leaving our drinks on the bar, I led her through the gathering crowd, scowling at anyone who didn't get the fuck out of my way, toward the door.

"What's he going to do?" Wesley asked, following us. "He can't protect you. Not from me, and certainly not from you."

The motherfucker had moved from taunting her to taunting me, and no way would I stand there and let him question my ability to protect anyone. Julia might not want to cause a scene at her sister's wedding, but I had no such qualms. Ready to swing, I spun around, but Julia intercepted me.

Her eyes were watering. "Please don't," she whispered, staring up at me.

Fuck.

"You going to hit me?" Wesley asked, too stupid to know when to stop. "You going to beat the shit out of me like you did Noah? Well, asshole, you can't jump me from behind like you did him. I'm ready for you."

One hit. That's all it would take. One hit and I could rearrange his jaw and shut him up for good.

Julia's eyes pleaded with me every bit as much as her mouth as she said, "He's not worth it. Please get me out of here."

As much as I hated to do so, I walked away from that fight.

Julia needed me more than I needed to shut that motherfucker up. By the time we made it to the dance floor, her entire body was trembling. I held her close, and she pressed her face against my chest.

82

Wrapping my arms around her, I found the slow beat of the song and began swaying us along to the music. We stayed like that for a few beats while she calmed down.

Finally, she whispered, "I failed. I let him bait me."

"He's an asshole who knows how to pull your strings. You lost one battle, but not the war. You've got this. We'll get you through the wedding and you'll never have to come back here. You're doing great. Just a little while longer."

"Do you think he was telling the truth? That he—"

Grabbing her chin, I gently tugged until she was looking up at me. "It doesn't matter. He's trying to get you back any way he can. That bastard fights dirty, but you know what? So do I. And I don't lose."

Her eyes were gorgeous. Intense. Complicated. For the first time since I'd known her, she dropped her guard and let me see what was behind her hard exterior, and it was beautiful. Soft. Delicate. Volatile. Dangerous. I saw her teetering between who she had been and who she wanted to be, battling the bonds that held her to the past. Her strength was breathtaking.

"Everyone's staring at us," she whispered.

Our feet had stopped, and we were standing in the middle of the dance floor. I glanced around, glaring at anyone brave enough to meet my gaze before returning my attention to her. "I don't give a single fuck what these people think, and you shouldn't either. I see you, Jules, and I know who you really are. You're better than this shit."

She swallowed, and more tears flooded her eyes, but she blinked them away. Did she ever allow herself to cry? Not in front of this group. Maybe not ever. I'd known her for less than a week and was probably the only one who'd ever seen her this real. This breakable. Life had turned her into a bitch, but that wasn't who she was. She was strong and beautiful and fierce.

I released her chin and she once again nestled against my chest.

"I don't want to be better," she muttered. "I want to kill him." But her tone lacked its previous seriousness. She'd turned the battle around.

"I know." I rubbed her back. "Bad idea, though."

"Why? Too many witnesses?"

I chuckled. "Definitely a concern."

She sucked in a deep breath and released it. Her body finally relaxed. "Thank you again for coming with me, Havoc. I couldn't have gotten through this without you."

Despite the situation, her bare skin beneath my hands and her big round tits pressed against me were making my dick take notice. There were several ways to fight for Julia, and like I'd told her, I fought dirty. I wasn't above fucking her senseless until she forgot all about this place and these people. "How long do we have to stick around?" I asked.

She glanced over her shoulder at the head table where Laura was busy chatting it up with the guests. "We'll go tell her goodbye after this dance."

8

Julia

"YOU'RE COLD," HAVOC said, eyeing my bare shoulders and arms.

It was a little after six p.m., and we were sitting on a mostly empty ferry, heading back to Seattle. We'd chosen a window booth, so we could watch the sun set behind the skyline of the city. The view was incredible, made more beautiful by the symbolism it presented. I'd survived Laura's wedding, and before the sun disappeared completely, I'd be done with this chapter of my life. I'd never have to return to Bainbridge Island, never have to see any of those assholes again.

I was finally free.

Previously unable to focus on anything past the wedding, I hadn't anticipated how cold the ferry would be on the way home. I should have brought a coat, and now I was paying for my shortsightedness. "I'm fine," I insisted.

"No lies, remember?" Havoc patted the bench seat beside him. "You're shivering. Come here."

As I scooted around the small table to join him, he removed his suit jacket and loosened his tie. Before I sat, he stood and draped his warm jacket over my shoulders, pulling it around me. It hung almost to my knees and smelled of wood, spices, and metal. Havoc's unique manly scent added to the warmth, making me feel safe and grounded. I snuggled into it and turned to return to my seat, but he patted the seat beside him again.

"Stay."

Etiquette and propriety be damned, I wanted to be near him. Wanted to be touching him. I sat, and he wrapped an arm around me and tucked me against his side.

"There. That's better."

He was so warm and strong I wanted to wrap myself around him and leech comfort like a parasite, but since we were still in public, this would have to do. People were already watching us, no doubt appalled by our display of public affection. We were coming from Bainbridge Island, after all, and the people there had standards. Moronic, lonely, stuffy standards.

"How're you doing?" Havoc asked.

"Still digesting the fact I lost control and threatened to kill my ex at my sister's wedding. So... peachy. Fantastic." I shook my head. "Should have never let him bait me like that. I gave him exactly what he wanted." But what bothered me the most was Wesley's revelation. Had he really plotted against me? Why? If he wanted to end our marriage, he should have said so. Why would he sleep with all my old friends? It was like he wanted to push me away. But then he'd mentioned watching me. Why would he push me away only to stalk me? Why wouldn't the asshole just leave me alone? The shiver I let out this time had nothing to do with the cold.

Havoc squeezed my shoulders. "It's over. You did great. You held it together, and we got the fuck out of there. That's all that matters."

I wasn't the only one who'd held it together. "Thank you for not grinding his face into the floor. As rewarding as it would be to watch Wesley get his cocky ass handed to him, I'm grateful that you walked away."

He shrugged. "Like you said... too many witnesses, and I'm trying to stay out of jail."

Giggling, I relaxed a little more. "I'm done talking about the wedding. Time for a subject change. Now that you've met my crazy family, tell me a little about yours."

Havoc didn't seem like the sharing type, but he surprised me and opened up about his mom and five sisters that all lived on the east coast. His parents had split when he was in middle school, and he and his sisters had gone back and forth between them until his father died his sophomore year of high school.

"Five sisters," I said. "I can't even imagine that. Growing up with Laura was bad enough."

"Five sisters and one bathroom." He shook his head. "It was savage."

One bathroom? I would have killed Laura for sure. "How did you guys get to school on time?"

"My parents didn't take any shit. If we acted up, we got the belt. It didn't stop us from acting up, but we got better about not getting caught."

My parents had never beat me, preferring to brainwash me and control my life instead. I think I would have preferred to be beaten. "Did you get the belt a lot?"

He nodded. "This'll probably surprise you, but I had a temper."

I gasped, pretending to be shocked. "You don't say?"

He chuckled. "Yeah, well, it's not as bad as yours, but it's significant."

I elbowed him in the side, and he grabbed my arm then trailed his fingers down the back of my hand. The gesture was strangely intimate.

"My sisters would fuck with me until I snapped, then they'd go crying to Dad. But trust me, they gave way better than I did. Half of my scars are from those diabolical tyrants."

"And the other scars?" I asked.

His expression darkened, and the arm wrapped around me stiffened. "I don't talk about those."

Havoc was a soldier. Although I'd spent the past year battling my inner bitch while keeping my family and ex at bay, I knew it was nothing compared to the combat Havoc had seen. How many scars had his time in the service given him? How many of those scars were tangible? I wanted to ask, but could tell the topic was off limits and didn't want him to clam up, so I veered around it.

"What made you enlist in the army?" I asked instead.

"Nine-eleven. The day I watched those planes fly into the twin towers, I knew I would serve. Then I forgot about it and focused on getting through high school. After graduation, I didn't have many options. Colleges don't exactly seek out broke inner-city kids, and I didn't know the first thing about applying for scholarships. Nobody in my family did. Besides, I'd been hangin' with a pretty rough crowd and was doing some stupid shit to help my mom keep food on the table. Spent a couple nights in juvie my senior year. My grades were good, but with a record... I knew if I didn't get the fuck out of there, I'd end up in prison."

There it was again. No games, no lies, no bullshit. Havoc was comfortable enough in his own skin that he could be honest about his life. His mouth was not a bakery, and he laid out the facts raw with no sugar to sweeten them up. He wasn't trying to impress me. He was letting me see the real him, scars, blemishes, criminal record, and all.

"You said your family is on the east coast. How'd you end up in Seattle?" I asked.

"Link." He grinned, and an incredible amount of pride shone through his eyes. "That's my man right there. He's the president of our motorcycle club and he was my Special Forces commander. No better motherfucker on the planet. He wouldn't shut up about this club his father had put together—a club for vets who helped other vets—and didn't give me much choice in the matter." Havoc chuckled. "He's one bossy son-of-a-bitch, but I guess that's what makes him a good president. His logic is solid, and his goals are good, so you find yourself doing whatever you can to help him succeed. He's the first person I ever met who believes in me. Really believes in me."

"Sounds like a great guy."

Havoc squeezed my shoulders again. "The best. But I've been wagging my jaw enough. Tell me more about you. Your mom said you had a degree. In what?"

Learning about Havoc was nice, and I wasn't ready for the conversation to come back around to my disaster of a life. But he'd shared a great deal of personal information, so I relented, willing to do the same. "Psychology. I knew I was screwed up and thought maybe I could fix myself. Instead, it made me better at screwing with other people. Taught me to look for their weaknesses and insecurities so I could better exploit them. Taught me to pay attention to what people *don't* say, so I know what areas of their lives to poke."

"Now you have a way to help people, though," he pointed out.

I stared at him, trying to follow his thinking. "It's weird how your mind automatically goes there," I said. "You're legitimately a good human and it's so bizarre. I don't know what to make of it."

"Don't put me on a pedestal, Jules. I already told you, I'm no saint." He frowned and looked away, out the window toward the city. "You wouldn't believe some of the shit I've done. Trust me, I've got my own demons."

That might be true, but he was still the best person I'd ever met. And... Jules? What was that about? Nobody had ever given me a nickname before. Well, other than bitch. And in high school, some peon had called me a cunt and then retracted it, insisting I lacked the necessary warmth and depth. That was my personal favorite jab. Insults I could handle. Pet names... those were too personal, too casual, too... warm and fuzzy for my comfort. But for some reason, Havoc calling me 'Jules' and 'Babe' made me want to arch my back, purring as I rubbed against him.

It made me want to be a better person. Someone he could respect and want to be around.

"Regardless, let's not put me in charge of anyone's mind," I said. "At least not until we're ready to build an army and take over the world."

He chuckled. "Noted."

With his arm still around me, we sat in companionable silence for the rest of the trip. By the time we docked and made our way to Havoc's truck, my buzz had worn off and I was back to wondering why Wesley had set me up and whether he was keeping tabs on me. Even after all this time, he could still weasel his way into my brain and screw with my thoughts, making me feel stupid and vulnerable. I didn't relish the idea of going back to my lonely apartment to let his words eat away at me until I popped enough sleeping pills to find oblivion.

"You okay?" Havoc asked as he pulled into the parking lot behind my bookstore.

I started to nod, but the look he gave me reminded me of our pact and I stopped myself. I wouldn't lie to him. "Can't stop thinking about what that vexatious little piss ant said. This entire past year, I thought *he* was the stupid one who'd screwed up. What if *I* was the stupid one, never questioning why he pushed me away? I've never considered Wesley a threat. With a few well-placed rumors and well-made alliances, I used to be able to take anyone down. But what if he *was* just playing me the whole time?"

Havoc stared at me for a few minutes before climbing out of his truck and circling around to open my door. He hoisted me down, shut the door, and then leaned me against it, trapping me between his massive body and the side of the truck.

"I'm gonna kiss you now," he said. "Okay?"

Shocked, I stared at him. Kiss me? Uh... "Okay."

He rested a hand on either side of my head and leaned in. I closed my eyes and welcomed his warm lips. As I opened up to him, his body pressed against me. He stroked the inside of my mouth, silently delivering promises I knew the growing bulge pressed against my stomach could deliver. His big, muscular body surrounded me, overpowering all my thoughts and senses with warmth and want. All I could see, hear, feel, taste, or think about was Havoc, and I reveled in how safe and protected his presence made me feel. But all too soon, he pulled away.

"How's your mind now?" he asked, pressing his erection harder against me.

All thoughts of Wesley had evaporated in a cloud of need and instinct. "Unnecessary," I replied. I didn't need a brain for the things I wanted to do to Havoc. For the things I wanted him to do to me.

"Want me to come up?" he asked with a smirk. If my panties weren't so damp from his kiss, that sexy, knowing smirk would have set them on fire. His hand cupped the side of my face and his thumb stroked my bottom lip. "I could keep that mind of yours preoccupied."

Instinct told me I should play hard to get, flirting coyly or something, but this no lies, no games, no bullshit concept was growing on me. "Yes. I would like that very much."

Havoc grinned and gave me one more kiss before releasing me and following me into my apartment. The distance between us cooled down my body, calmed my libido, and jump-started my nerves. Having never been with anyone other than Wesley (and that was over a year ago), I had no clue what to expect. Havoc was little more than a stranger, and probably the closest thing to an actual friend I'd ever had. It was a weird combination, and I didn't know how to proceed. I needed his body. The attraction between us was too strong to deny. I wanted to do all the beautiful, dirty things I read about in my romance novels with him, but I also didn't want this to be a wham-bam-thank-you-ma'am situation. If I let him fuck me, would I ever see him again?

Could I let him walk out of my life?

The idea of it was staggeringly painful, which made no sense at all. I needed to numb that shitty feeling and muster up some courage, so I headed for the kitchen. "Can I get you a drink?" I asked.

"Sure. What do you got?"

Looking over the contents of my refrigerator, I replied, "How about rum and guava?"

"Never had it."

"It's like a tropical paradise in your mouth. Complete with sexy pirates, and I'll decorate it with one of those cute little umbrellas."

He chuckled. "Babe, I got a rep to uphold. I'll try the drink, but pass on the pirates and umbrellas."

"Spoil sport. Make yourself comfortable. I'll be out in a minute." I pulled glasses out of the cupboard, made us each a drink, sucked down half of mine, refilled it, and headed out to the living room.

Havoc was lounging on my sofa, looking far sexier than any man had a right to. He'd removed his shoes, tie, and shirt, revealing the tight white tank stretched across his impressive pecks and abs in a drool-worthy display of hotness. As I checked him out, he gave me that knowing smirk again.

"You said to get comfortable."

Yes. Yes, I had, and oh boy was I enjoying the eye candy that request had produced. I handed him his drink and then took another giant gulp of my own before shedding his suit jacket. The liquor was already warming me up and dampening my inhibitions. I hung the jacket over the back of the recliner and sucked down more of my drink.

"How're you doing?" he asked, eyeing my glass as he sipped from his own. He patted the cushion beside him. "You seem keyed up. Sit. Talk to me." He took another sip. "This shit isn't bad."

No, it was good. Strong. Perfect. My buzz was already coming back, and soon I'd be good to go, ready to make rash decisions I'd most likely regret tomorrow in a desperate attempt to feel better tonight. Draining the rest of my glass, I stood. "I'm gonna make another."

I turned to go back into the kitchen, but Havoc

94

grabbed my hand, halting my progress. "No, babe. You're not getting shit-faced."

Who the hell was he to cut me off in my own house? Before I could tell him to mind his own business and take advantage of me like I needed him to, he tugged me down onto his lap. "You're nervous. I get that. But if you let me, I can make you feel better." The back of his hand trailed up my bare arm, leaving goosebumps in its wake. As his hard cock pressed against my backside, he slowly removed the pins from my hair, releasing it in a cascade of curls. His eyes darkened, and his fingers ran through my hair and trailed down my bare back as his lips landed on mine. He grabbed my arms and held me still, kissing my breath away. His hands continued to roam my body, sliding down my cleavage, kneading my breasts, slipping under my dress and to climb my thighs to my hot, wet core. Pushing aside my thong, he teased my folds, and I moaned into his mouth. With his fingers still dancing over my sensitive nub, he pulled back and met my gaze, his expression dangerous. It sent a thrill up my spine and more heat to my core.

"I can help you, Jules."

He'd already done so much, yet, I would gladly accept more. "How?"

"I'll make you scream my name so many times you'll forget his." He plucked the glass from my hand and set it down on the coffee table. "But only if you're sober. We're not doing this if you're wasted."

I swallowed and looked away from his soul-consuming stare. "And afterward? I know it's lame, but you're... I've really enjoyed spending time with you, and..." My god, I sounded so weak! Wanting to kick myself, I snapped my mouth closed, hoping I hadn't screwed this up.

"I'm not going anywhere, babe." He stroked my hair out of my face, tucking it behind my ears.

Relieved, I let out a breath. "How do you feel about us being friends? With benefits?"

His lips grazed my jaw then drifted down my neck as his hand continued to massage my most sensitive area. "If that's what you want, I'm in, but I have a couple of conditions."

What was it with this guy and his conditions? His fingers and lips were driving me so crazy I probably would have agreed to anything as long as he kept it up. "I'm listening."

"No lying, no games,"

"No bullshit," I finished.

"Right. You gotta keep being straight with me." His finger circled my entrance before dipping into me.

I moaned, nodding. "Yes. Okay."

"Good." He pulled his finger out and spread my wetness around my clit. "We need to be exclusive. Everyone has their triggers, and that's mine, Jules. I don't fuck around, and if I'm hittin' this pussy and I find out you let some other motherfucker in, I'll probably snap and kill him. I don't share. Ever."

The idea of him killing for me probably shouldn't turn me on, but it did. The passion in his jealousy was so hot it made me want to wrap my legs around him. "Never mastered those sandbox skills, did ya?" The words came out breathy, husky.

"My sandbox, my toys." He dipped his finger inside me again while nibbling my neck and I almost came.

"Yes," I breathed, agreeing to his conditions and the incredible things he was doing to my body. "But it goes both ways. I will cut a bitch, Havoc. I will chop her up into little pieces and they will never find her body."

"Fuck," he pulled his hand away from my core to cradle me in his arms, standing. My jealousy must have turned him on as well. "I need to be inside of you. Now. Where's your bed?"

I directed him to the door, and he marched right in and set me beside the bed. "I love this dress, but it's gotta go," he said, bending to grab the hem of my gown and pull it over my head in one smooth motion before tossing it aside. His gaze raked over my body before landing on the cups holding up my boobs. "You're gonna have to help me out here."

While I removed the cups, Havoc went to work on the rest of my body. He kissed my stomach and my hips as he slid my thong down and had me step out of it. Finished with the bra cups, I leaned over to undo the straps of my heels, but he stopped me.

"Leave them," he commanded. Then his gaze landed on my breasts which were a little red from the adhesive on the cups. "Does that hurt?" he asked.

I shook my head. Between the booze and what he was doing to my body, I felt nothing but pleasure.

"You have the sexiest tits I've ever seen," he said, grabbing one as his mouth attacked the other. His other hand snaked around my waist and palmed my ass, holding me against him while he sucked and played. He released my nipple to attack the other one before pulling away to let his gaze drift further south.

"You ready for this, Jules?" he asked.

I nodded. But since he wasn't looking at my face, I added, "Yes."

Attention still on my pussy, he licked his lips. "Good, because I'm fuckin' hungry and you look delicious."

9

Havoc

J ULIA'S BODY WAS incredible, soft and hard in all the right places. It responded to every touch, every kiss. I couldn't wait to see how she reacted to my cock. I'd never been so turned on in my life, and it was a struggle not to throw her on the bed and slam my dick into her. I promised her multiple orgasms, though, and I'm nothing if not a man of my word.

With my back to the bed, I knelt in front of Julia, running my hands down her perfect body. She watched with hooded eyes as I spread her legs and scooted her forward until she was straddling my face. I started with a gentle lick from entrance to clit, and she moaned and rested her hands on the bed behind me for support. I licked again and again before focusing on that little nub of nerves, reaching up to pinch her nipples while I sucked and teased her. Once her clit was fully swollen, I ran my tongue down her seam before plunging into her soaked pussy. She tasted so sweet I wanted more, and the way her body was trembling encouraged me to go deeper.

"Fuck my face, Jules," I demanded. "You're so sweet. I want to taste you when you come."

With my tongue back inside her, I draped her legs over my shoulders and leaned my head back onto the bed. I grabbed her ass and scooted her forward again, so I could get deeper. Her body was reacting, but she was holding back. Still trying to be so goddamn prim and proper. That's okay. I knew how to force her to let go. Torturing us both, I slid my tongue out of her pussy and went back to gently licking her clit.

She growled in frustration.

I laughed. "What's wrong, babe?" I licked her again. "Not what you want?"

"No."

"Tell me." My hands slid up the inside of her thighs until I positioned my thumbs at either side of her entrance.

"I want... you to... go back to what you were doing."

"You want me to stick my tongue back in your pussy?"

"Yes."

"Say the words, Jules. Tell me what you want."

"Put your tongue in me."

She wasn't getting off that easily. "In where? Talk dirty to me."

"Put your tongue in my pussy."

"Only if you promise to use it. Promise to fuck

my mouth?" I blew on her entrance, and then circled it with my tongue, giving her a little incentive.

She moaned. "Yes."

"The words, babe."

"I'll fuck your mouth."

Damn, her voice was sexy. When my tongue plunged back in, she cried out in relief. She didn't move, but I couldn't stop. My dick was getting impatient, and I needed her to come so I could fuck her and find my release. I grabbed her hips and started grinding her against my face. She picked up on what I was doing and took over, getting me deeper into that spot she needed me in. It was so fucking hot to watch her as she worked to pleasure herself on my tongue. I moved my hands to her ass to give her a little more stability, and she responded with fervor, picking up the pace until she unraveled around me. When she was done, I flipped her over, lying her on the bed to lap up the last of her juices.

"You taste so damn good," I said, removing my tank.

Her eyes cracked open, and she stared at my chest approvingly. Her appreciation only made me harder. She watched as I grabbed a condom from my pocket and set it on the bed before unfastening my belt and pants and sliding them down. Her gaze went straight to the bulge in my boxers, so I stroked it before removing the last of my clothing and setting my cock free. Her eyes widened as she stared at it.

"What's on your mind, Jules?" I asked, rolling the condom over my cock.

"That is... uh... I'm concerned about it fitting. I mean... daaayum."

I grabbed her by the waist and scooted her until her ass teetered on the edge of the bed. To make sure she was still ready for me, I bent and lapped at her pussy one more time as I rolled on the condom. She was even wetter. "Tastes like you like my big dick," I said. "Your pussy's ready for it."

Leaning over her body, I sucked a nipple into my mouth and lined my cock up at her entrance. She was so damn tight it took every ounce of control I had not to come as I eased my way inside her, watching the perfect contrast of my black cock disappearing into her pale entrance. It was the hottest thing I'd ever seen. Refusing to blow my load, I thought about football and forced my body to calm the fuck down. Julia wasn't helping matters with her sexy lip biting and sensual little mewling sounds. I wanted to fuck her harder. Faster.

Friends with benefits.

If that's what she needed from me, that's what we'd be. For now. But as I eased deeper into her tight pussy, with the sweet taste of her still on my tongue, I planned to hit this as many times as she let me. I felt feral. Possessed. I wanted to claim her... to make sure she knew her pussy was mine and only mine. To fuck her until she walked bowlegged. I wanted to show her positions and challenge her sexually in ways that her ex could only dream of.

The fucker had gotten into my head, too, but I'd show him I could protect her. Even from herself.

Pulling out of Julia, I draped her legs over my shoulders before pumping back inside. Deeper now. She took me all in. Her big round tits bounced, and she let out a gasp. Creamy skin writhing on her gray comforter, legs in the air, hair spread out like a goddamn halo, she looked like a fucking dream.

Her pussy squeezed around my dick, and I sucked in a breath. I'd never been inside something so tight and perfect.

"Oh God," she breathed, arching her back.

Those tits. I wanted my cock squeezed between them. If I could clone myself, I would take every inch of her body at once. I'd slam my dick into her mouth, her pussy, and her ass as my hands and lips memorized her body. She was mine, and I wanted all of her.

"You like that?" I asked, sliding out to slam back into her, harder. "Like it when I fuck you, Jules?"

Her walls tightened around me again as her climax built. "Yes."

No way was I letting her come again so soon. Time to tease her a bit. I pulled out completely and attacked her tits with my mouth.

She growled again, like a cute little kitten playing with a dangerous grizzly. She could growl all she wanted, but I'd already eaten her, and now I was toying with my food. Chuckling at her mock ferociousness, I released her nipple to claim her mouth, letting her taste herself on my tongue. Growling and writhing, she grabbed a hold of my cock and tried to force me back into her.

Releasing her mouth, I asked, "What do you want, babe?" I dipped the head inside her and stilled. Soaked. Hot. My dick ached to go all the way in, to spread her wide and fuck her the way she wanted me to. "Do you want this?"

"Yes."

"You know I like it when those perfect plump lips talk dirty. Tell me what you want. Be explicit." I pulled out of her again.

Another growl. "I want your cock."

I sucked on her nipple, nibbling until she gasped. "How do you want it?"

"I want you to fuck me," she breathed. "Hard. Fuck me hard, Havoc."

That, I could do. I scooped her up by the waist, positioned her higher on the bed, and flipped her over on her hands and knees. "Is this how you want it?" I asked.

"Yes," she breathed.

I grabbed her hips, and buried myself deep inside her in one hard thrust.

She gasped.

"How hard do you want it?" I asked.

"Harder," she said. "Faster."

Not only was she gorgeous, tough, smart, and funny, but she liked it rough. I was in heaven. Digging my hand in her hair, I gave a little tug as I picked up the pace. "You like that?"

"Yes. God, yes. Fuck me."

Our skin slapped together as I pumped into her. With my free hand, I smacked her ass, gently at first.

"More," she cried out.

I smacked her harder, again and again, until her ass cheek was red. Then I released her hair and changed hands to start in on the other side.

"God, yes," she whimpered.

Her pussy squeezed around me again and I almost lost control. I needed to get her there before I did. I reddened up the other ass cheek. She let out a moan and then her walls squeezed around me again. She was close.

"Good girl. Come for me. Get there."

Grabbing a hold of her hips I fucked her until we both cried out our release. She collapsed on the bed, and I stood to get rid of the condom. I washed up and came back to her bedroom, wondering what I should do. I was damn tired, and her king-sized bed looked comfortable and inviting, especially with the blanket down around her hips. Bet I could sleep really well cupping her tits in my hands. Maybe with a nipple in my mouth...

But Julia and I were in a good place—friends with benefits, fuck yeah!—and I didn't want shit between us to get complicated. The last time I'd spent the night had landed me with a clinger that had taken forever to shake.

Not like I had any intention of shaking Julia. No, I was far from finished with her tight little pussy. But that was beside the point. She had established boundaries, and I wanted to respect what she'd decided. Friends with benefits. I'd respect the shit out of that. And hopefully, in return, she'd be willing to let me pound that pussy often. Which led me to the question I was struggling with... Did friends sleep over in the same bed? Not damn likely. I reached for my pants, but before I could put them on she opened one eye and stared at me.

"Stay," she said, her voice heavy with sleep. "You didn't make me scream your name once, so you still have work to do." Smiling, her eyelid closed, and she patted the bed beside her.

This broad was dangerous; she knew how to pull my strings. No way could I walk out after she'd laid down a challenge like that. Planning for an eventful night, I tugged the rest of the condoms from my pocket and set them on the nightstand for easy access. Then I slid into bed beside her. Julia was already asleep, so I relaxed, resting before round two. Because there would be a round two. I passed out on my side, spooning her sexy body and palming one of her perfect tits.

A few hours later, I woke up on my back with Julia's lips wrapped around my dick. "Good morning," she garbled around a mouthful of cock. Then she smiled and slid down my shaft until I hit the back of her throat.

Best fucking wake-up call I'd ever had. I moaned, pushing myself deeper. She practically swallowed my cock whole before coming back up.

"That feels so fuckin' good," I hissed.

Smiling, she did her best to swallow me again. I watched, admiring the contrast of her pink lips sliding up and down my shaft. The way she hollowed out her cheeks to get further. The way her eyes watered with the effort.

"You are so damn sexy, Jules."

She released my shaft and attacked my balls, sucking one into her mouth, and then the other. When she finished, she fanned out her tongue and slowly licked up my shaft from base to head. She was killing me. I let her play for a while, and then it was time for revenge.

"Swing your hips over here," I commanded. "I want your pussy."

She shook her head. "Nope. This is all about you. You know I like it when those perfect plump lips talk dirty. Tell me what you want. Be explicit."

The smartass was throwing my words back at me. Thought she was in charge, did she? Cute. Time to remind the little kitten what it felt like to be devoured. I grabbed her by the hips and positioned her to straddle my face.

"Hey!" she objected.

My tongue landed on her clit and her argument morphed into a moan. I licked and flicked, and she went back to sucking on my cock. Her pussy was already soaked. Sucking my dick had turned her on, and I loved that. Desperate to repay the morning oral she'd blessed me with, I alternated between fingering and licking her. Her mouth slid up and down my cock. She added both hands. Rubbing. Tugging. I licked her harder, faster, my fingers attacking her g-spot as I worked. It became a competition. The harder and faster I fucked her with my tongue and fingers, the harder and faster she sucked my dick. Soon, her head was bobbing up and down so fast my balls were clenching as I tried not to blow my load. With my fingers and tongue still plunging into her pussy, I tried to pull my dick out of her mouth, but she refused to give it up.

I came in her mouth and she fucking swallowed it!

I would have never pegged a girl like Julia for a swallower, but it only made me appreciate her more. Determined to show her my gratitude, I flipped her over, so I was on top. Then I repositioned myself and ate her pussy until she screamed my name, begging me to stop because she was ticklish after coming. We settled into bed again, and I glanced at the alarm clock. Four forty-three a.m.

"Do you have to go?" she asked, sounding disappointed as she followed my gaze. "Because that was only once, and you cheated by tickling me. You promised I'd be screaming your name many times. One is not many."

She'd lowered the blanket to her waist, revealing her beautiful tits. She'd figured out my weakness and now she was using it against me. Shaking my head, I let out a chuckle before motor-boating the hell out of her tits. She laughed, begging me to stop.

"That's twice, babe. I already told you, I fight dirty."

It was Sunday, and this was my weekend off. I had all kinds of shit to do around my house, but the naked little vixen lying beside me was already making me hard again. Sucking a big, dark red nipple into my mouth, I reached for another condom.

We alternated between fucking and napping until it was time for Julia to get up and get ready for work. Then we showered, dressed, and I walked her down to the shop and gave her a kiss goodbye before heading out. I didn't know whether it was appropriate for friends to kiss goodbye, but I also didn't give a shit.

10

Julia

R EGRET. THAT'S WHAT I expected to feel after the wild, passionate night of casual sex I experienced with Havoc. Instead, I felt wonderful, invigorated, and sore. Holy crap, was I ever sore. That man and his giant penis had worked me over good, and I'd loved every minute. He walked me down to work and kissed me goodbye—which was a pleasant surprise—before heading out. And now I was buzzing around the bookstore, straightening shelves, dusting away cobwebs, and looking for woodland critters to sing to because I was sure this had to be a fairytale. Only my prince was a friendly neighborhood biker with his club logo tattooed on his chest. Hung like a horse, he stayed hard like an alligator. Seriously. I'd read that alligators have constant erections, and last night, Havoc had been one glorious reptile.

That last thought was questionable, but I was on

cloud nine, and the oxygen was thin, making me ridiculously giddy. I picked up my cell phone to call Laura and brag about my incredible night, but remembered that she was on her way to the Caribbean for her ten-day honeymoon. Damn. I finally had juicy details to share and nobody to share them with.

I needed friends.

So far, I had one friend, and he was the reason I was walking funny. Maybe I should tell him how great last night was? I picked up my phone and considered it, but he'd only been gone for a couple of hours and I didn't want to appear desperate. Wasn't there some rule about waiting and making the guy text first? That sounded like a game, which violated one of Havoc's conditions, so I should probably just be honest and let him know how he rocked my world. Before I could change my mind, I sent him a quick message to let him know I had fun last night. Fun. Talk about an understatement.

A couple of customers came in and I greeted them and pointed out the sci-fi/fantasy section before checking my phone for a reply. Nothing. I put away my phone and rang up the customers before checking again. Still no text back. My stomach churned, second guessing my text. Second guessing everything we'd shared last night. He'd been so sweet and wonderful at the wedding and on the ferry. It felt like we'd connected. Had I screwed up everything by letting him into my bed?

What if he didn't enjoy it?

What if he was just another horny asshole who'd played me for sex?

He himself had told me he was no saint. Was that his way of letting me know he'd bounce after we did the deed?

I'd been wrong about Wesley. What if I was wrong about Havoc, too?

Stop.

I had to get out of my mind or I'd go crazy. It was too soon to assume anything about Havoc. He'd seemed genuine, so I shouldn't be so quick to judge him. He was probably preoccupied and would text me back when he got the chance. The world didn't revolve around my stupid insecurities and need for an immediate response. Why was I staring at my phone like a paranoid lunatic? Desperate to stay busy so I wouldn't think about it, I pulled out a bottle of cleaner and went to work shining up the storefront windows. Then I wiped down the mirror in the bathroom and dusted all the framed art. By the time lunch came around, the store was practically sparkling; it was so clean. I checked my phone for a response from Havoc and instead found a text from an unknown number. Frowning, I clicked it open.

'You looked amazing yesterday. I miss you. Can we meet up and talk?'

Definitely not the text I was hoping for. I typed out several creative suggestions for how Wesley could die before erasing them all and choosing not to respond. I was still contemplating the benefits of killing the irredeemable fuckwit, and if I actually snapped and went through with that course of action, I didn't want to leave any evidence.

My phone beeped with another incoming text.

'Has Havoc told you our little secret yet? Or is he seeing how many more times he can get you to scream his name, first?'

As I read the text, ice flooded my veins and little warning bells went off in my mind. I read it again and again, trying to deny the implications. Wesley knew about Havoc's challenge. How? There was only one obvious answer, and it flitted around in my brain waiting for me to grasp it, but I refused. I'd just had the most amazing night of my life and I couldn't accept that it had all been a setup.

There had to be another explanation, but I couldn't think of one.

Tears stung my eyes.

Refusing to let them fall, I blinked them away and looked at my phone again. Still no response from Havoc. Or maybe this was his response. Admission by silence.

I wanted to text Havoc and ask him point-blank if he'd told Wesley about us. No, I wanted to call him, so I could spit out any lies he tried to feed me. But the two of them would just love that, wouldn't they? I bet they couldn't wait for me to call Havoc, crying, admitting what a fool I'd been. Not this bitch.

Pieces were fitting into place, creating a picture I couldn't deny. Havoc had conveniently shown up right when I needed him. After I'd told my sister I'd take him to her wedding. Could Laura be in on this? The thought sliced open my heart, and a sob bubbled out of my chest. No. And yet... I couldn't rule anything out. Wesley trying to provoke Havoc at the wedding... all for show. No wonder Havoc walked away so easily. Some "helper of the city" he turned out to be. I bet he was laughing his ass off when I asked to be friends with benefits. All his talk about being exclusive...

Shit.

Was Havoc somewhere laughing himself silly over my stupid, gullible ass? Maybe sharing a beer with Wesley at some skeezy watering hole?

Wesley. I should have seen this coming. That bastard and I had been separated for more than a year and divorced for ten months and thirteen days. He'd let me walk out of his life with nothing more than a wave goodbye. It had been too easy. Wesley was far too possessive and vindictive to let anyone, or anything, go. Still, he hadn't fought for me. He hadn't even bullied me into coming back, and he could have.

'Why are you doing this?' I typed to Wesley. I had to know, hoping that the knowledge would help ease the pain of Havoc's betrayal.

Seconds later, my phone pinged with his response. 'Why do you think? You're mine, Julia. You've always been mine.'

I don't know what I'd been expecting, but that wasn't it. 'You let me go. No, you pushed me away.' I replied.

'I changed my mind.'

While I stared at the words, trying to deny the way they twisted my insides and tied my shoulders in knots, Justine came in and plopped her backpack on the counter. I felt her gaze on me as she asked, "You okay?"

No. Definitely not. I thought I'd escaped, but

now I was back on Wesley's radar. No, I was the center of his bullseye. And he wasn't the stupid weakling I'd taken him for. I couldn't take him down. Hell, I couldn't even counter his attacks. I'd been foolish and conceited to believe I was so much smarter and better at the game than he was.

Wesley was actually a threat.

But truth be told, he wasn't the one tearing me up inside.

Havoc had kissed me goodbye.

Had he immediately betrayed me to Wesley, or had he kicked the idea around for a while first?

"Julia?" Justine sounded worried.

The gallon of coffee I'd consumed throughout the day was threatening to come back up. "I need a minute. Man the store?"

Before Justine could answer, I grabbed my phone and hurried toward the stairs in the back and up to my apartment.

Tucked behind the ibuprofen in my bathroom cabinet was a prescription for some sort of anti-psychotic Mom had started me on in middle school. It was for anxiety or paranoia or some other ailment I didn't have but knew which answers to give to convince a doctor I did.

"It will make you feel better," Mom had promised.

What she meant was that it would make me feel nothing. And nothing was currently what I needed to feel. The number of emotions spiraling out of control in my head was crippling. If I didn't find a way to mute them, I'd go crazy. Then I'd throw my idiotic, gullible self off a roof. I needed to think, not feel. Careful not to look into my bedroom and drudge up memories of Havoc on my bed, I went straight to the bathroom and tossed two pills back. Then I headed to the kitchen for a drink of water, which I immediately upgraded to rum. Alcohol was just the catalyst I needed to help the numbness kick in faster. Screw warning labels; they didn't understand the emotional barrage I was dealing with here. Once I was sufficiently self-medicated, I dragged myself into the living room and collapsed on the recliner and pulled a faded five-by-seven photograph of paradise from the hollow book on top of the coffee table.

Focusing on the image until I set it in my mind, I closed my eyes and attempted to go there in my mind.

Havoc's sexy smirk was all I saw.

Swearing, I shook my head and focused on the picture before trying again. Still no luck. I pulled the saltwater breeze candle from my coffee table drawer and lit it. By the time the fragrance filled the room, the pills and rum were kicking in. I inhaled deeply through my nose and closed my eyes again.

Finally, I found myself standing on the Nā Pali Coastline of Kauai. The lush, rocky hiking trail clung to the side of the mountain, giving a breathtaking view of both the vast, blue ocean, and the rugged terrain. This was always the one place in my mind where I could find peace and quiet. The one happy memory I could count on. I was just a child with my Hawaiian nanny, visiting her family for a wedding. The festivities had been fun, but this trail was what I remembered the most. As I stood on the cliffs watching the dark forms of sea life swam beneath my feet, I felt so small. So insignificant. Free. I had no control of anything.

In this spot, I could be anything I wanted.

The memory of Havoc's sexy smirk tugged at my subconscious again, stinging my eyes and creating a lump in my throat. I'd trusted him. We'd connected.

It was all a lie.

On this cliff, I was also alone. Nobody could hurt me while I was alone.

Taking a deep breath, I pushed thoughts of Havoc and what could have been away and refocused, finding peace and safety once again. This temporary freedom was what my psychology degree had earned me. Following the techniques I'd learned, I imagined ripping each pesky emotion from my body and casting them into the dark forms below. The fish swam out to sea, taking my pain, anger, and hurt beyond the horizon. I had so much to give... so many feelings. By the time the last fish disappeared, carrying away the sting of Havoc's betrayal, I felt numb.

I'd survive.

Sucked down deep breaths through my nose, I stood. I'd made a mistake and let someone in. No big deal. It happened. Now, it was time to rectify the situation. Desperate to remove all traces of Havoc and my misjudgment, I extinguished the saltwater candle and lit other scents, scattering them around my house. Then, I stripped the sheets from my bed and spritzed the sofa where he'd sat.

"I'll make you scream my name so many times you'll forget his."

The memory blindsided me, stealing the breath from my lungs. Closing my eyes, I fed it to the fish and then proceeded to give my apartment the same treatment I'd given the bookstore.

While I was steam mopping my kitchen, Havoc called. My entire body froze as I stared at the phone, wondering if I should answer. The feelings I'd sent away started returning. Memories of the heat of his body as he tucked me under his arm on the ferry burned away the top layer of my resolve. He'd been so sweet, so perfect, was it all fake? The possibility sent cracks of pain through my entire existence.

I'd let Havoc in.

I'd told him shit I'd never told anyone, allowing him to see what was beneath the surface. He'd stripped away my lies and manipulations until I stood naked in front of him. If he turned out to be just another mind fuck, courtesy of Wesley, it would break me. And not even the Nā Pali Coastline would put me back together again.

Our time together had been sizzling hot and incredibly fun, but I was far too flammable to play with fire.

I let the call go to voicemail.

Knowing I needed to block his number to avoid temptation, I opened up the commands on my recent call and hovered over the "block number" option.

"Come on, Jules, this should be easy," I muttered to myself. The pep talk didn't work. Despite all my reservations, all my returning fear, distrust, and insecurities, I wasn't ready to let Havoc go.

What if he's innocent?

Frustrated, I plopped my phone back on the counter and went to go take another little white pill.

11

Havoc

JULIA WAS GHOSTING my phone calls. I let it slide for a few days, giving her time to come to grips with all the shit that had gone down during the wedding and after. But now, it was Wednesday evening and my patience had come to a screeching halt.

My day started with the same nightmare I'd had hundreds of times. I was back in Syria, staring into the hollow, accusatory eyes of a kid holding his mom. Only this time, his mom was a redhead with bright green eyes. Recognizing Julia, I raced to her side and ripped off my shirt, pressing it to her bullet wound to staunch the flow of blood. Julia grabbed my hand and whispered something. I couldn't hear her, so I got closer. Then the kid—that little fucker —shot me.

Wide awake at three-thirty a.m. because I couldn't get back to sleep after that shit, I tried to call Julia. She didn't answer, of course, and I'd narrowly resisted the urge to drive over there and beat on her door until she either let me in or called the cops. But I *did* resist. Then, when I got to work, some broad called and asked for a tow. Got the address and vehicle information and she promised to meet me there for the hookup. When I arrived on site, the broad wasn't there. As I waited for her to show, a man came out of the building and asked why I was casing his car. Like I was getting ready to steal the damn thing.

Turns out the spiteful bitch was trying to have her ex-boyfriend's car towed because of a nasty breakup.

Made me wonder if I'd dodged a bullet with Julia. Maybe shit was better this way. But why did I feel so fucked up over it?

After work, I headed to the station, parked my bike, and pulled out my phone to find a text from Julia. Excited, I opened it.

'Leave me alone.'

That was it.

How the hell did she go from 'I had fun last night' to 'Leave me alone'? What the fuck had I done?

Nothing. How could I do anything when she wouldn't even text or call me back?

It felt like she was playing me.

She'd promised no games, but nothing else made sense. Her family had fucked her up, but we'd made progress during and after the wedding and now... now I was beating my head against an invisible wall. Nothing was there. If she'd just answer one of my goddamn calls, I could talk some sense into her. I needed to see her but couldn't bring myself to go there uninvited. Not while one big question kept assaulting my brain.

Had she gone back to the asshole?

The possibility made me want to punch something. Preferably a rich little pencil-dicked asshat named Wesley. Frustrated, I slammed my phone into my pocket and climbed off my bike. I needed advice, and there was only one person I trusted to give it to me.

The common area of the station had its usual Wednesday night crowd. Some of the old guys were shooting pool and throwing darts while a dozen or so of the brothers huddled around the televisions, watching the game. Lacy (a cute little red-headed club whore) was going down on Zombie in the hallway right before the kitchen. Shaking my head, I stepped around them and went to the refrigerator to grab a couple of beers.

Don't get me wrong, I wasn't judging Zombie or Lacy. I'd spent my fair share of time with the club whores and had been on the receiving end of Lacy's talented mouth more than once and had no room to judge anyone. As Sage had pointed out, there was therapy in sex and when you were dealing with a bunch of half-cocked ex-soldiers, the physical and emotional release was necessary. But lately, the club whores didn't quite do it for me. I was looking for something... more. Not like I wanted to settle down or some shit like that, but I at least wanted a connection. Someone I could relate to and have as my own.

Someone I didn't have to share.

Julia and I had understood each other, and the

exclusive friends with benefits relationship she'd offered would have been perfect for us both. I enjoyed spending time with her and she was a mind-blowing fuck. We could have hung out and worked off tension without the drama and expectations placed on a dating relationship. It would have given us both a chance to test the waters and see if we could have handled something more between us. Then she had to go and put me on ignore.

Why? Had she given up the fight and returned to her own life? Or had she returned to take another shot at Wesley, and now she was sitting in a jail cell while I was losing my ever-lovin' mind over her?

Link's office door was open, which meant that he and Emily weren't in there getting it on (like they usually were when Link worked late. Those two were worse than a couple of fucking rabbits). I paused at the door and waited for him to invite me in. He stopped typing on his laptop and looked up at me questioningly.

"Hey brother. You look like a fuckin' storm cloud darkenin' my doorway. What's goin' on?" he asked.

Link had been my best friend since the Army. When I met him, we were training for the Q-course and thought we were hot shit. There are several misconceptions about Army Special Forces. Most common is that we're all like Rambo, flexing our bulging biceps as we single-handedly infiltrate and attack the enemy in savage bloodbaths while throwing out shitty one-liners. Nothing could be further from the truth. Although our A-Team saw its fair share of dangerous missions, we spent the majority of our time educating and training allies. We were all intelligent and well-trained with wiry, fit bodies that enabled us to run for days with little to no calories (AKA badass slender nerds). And most importantly, we don't do that solo bullshit; we work as a team.

My time in the service thinned me down, toughened me up, expanded my mind, and taught me to trust someone other than myself. My team was the shit, and every last one of them had my back. Link was more than my commander, though. His moral compass, integrity, and wisdom pushed me to be a good man while teaching me to forgive myself when I fell short. He was the brother I never had—the brother I chose—and I was glad to call him my president and my friend.

"You got a few minutes?" I asked, holding up the beers.

He pushed back from his computer and gestured at the couch on the other side of his desk. "Yeah, man. Come in. Have a seat and tell me what's got you lookin' so goddamn murderous."

Link had a bottle opener attached to the side of his desk. I used it to pop the tops off the beers and passed him one before making myself comfortable. Taking a long pull, I struggled to organize my thoughts. Nobody knew about Julia. Not a goddamn soul. I couldn't even put the experience into words. I'd been propositioned at a bookstore, took a perfect stranger to her sister's wedding, and now I was moping around like a little bitch because she hadn't called me back. I'd felt a genuine connection to Julia. Had it only been sex for her? I was a wreck inside and didn't want to open up at all, but Sage says that talking through shit often helps you categorize it and quantify its significance. I didn't know about all that, but if I didn't talk to someone soon, I'd explode. Link was doing the relationship thing with Emily, so if anyone would understand me, it was him.

"I know I'm one hell of a sexy beast, but are you gonna talk or just stare at me all day?" he asked.

Shaking my head, I replied, "Trying to figure you out, bro. What makes a girl like Emily fall for an ugly motherfucker like you?"

He grinned. "She sits on my face a lot."

"Way too much information, man."

"You asked."

"Consider me duly punished."

He nodded, watching me as he took a drink. "I take it this is about a woman."

That proved to be the opening I needed. Starting from the way Julia had practically eye-fucked me in her bookstore before trying to trick me into taking her to the wedding, I told him everything that had transpired between us. He listened quietly, often nodding. It felt strangely good to let it all out. The entire experience, from our first meeting to the morning I kissed her goodbye, felt like a tornado that had been swirling everything together in my mind. Talking through it allowed me to compartmentalize my interactions with Julia and look at each one for what it was. Regardless of her lack of response to my calls and texts, we had connected. I was sure of it. But that meant that something else was going on... something she didn't want to talk to me about.

Link listened until I finished, and then shook his head with a low chuckle. "You stayed the night?"

"Yeah. She's got a comfortable bed."

"And I bet all you did was snuggle." He laughed, waiting for me to defend myself.

I didn't. I wasn't lying when I said I didn't share, and that included details. Some shit was sacred and what happened in Julia's bedroom would stay between her and me.

"She must be one hell of a woman if she has *you* this fucked up." Link drained the last of his beer and set it on his desk in what felt like a signal, ending out conversation. "I can't wait to meet her."

That was it? I'd been expecting him to tell me she sounded crazy and that I needed to walk away from the drama before I did something stupid that landed me back in jail. Nothing could have prepared me for him complimenting her and wanting to meet her before dismissing me. Had he been listening?

"She's got all kinds of shit going on with her family and her ex. You heard that, right?" I asked. "She's given me an out by ignoring me. Hell, she told me to leave her alone. Maybe I should just forget about her."

He shrugged. "All right. Do that. Whatever." His attention went back to his laptop.

The idea of never seeing Julia again tied my stomach in knots and made me want to bust shit up. Why hadn't she called me back? Why the fuck was she messing with me like this? And why didn't Link give a shit? "What the fuck, man?" I asked.

"It was your suggestion."

"It was a shitty suggestion. I came to you because I was hoping for something else."

"You said it yourself... this broad is making you crazy. If you can walk away, then yeah, you should. Why not?"

Because she needed me. She had no friends, a horrible family, no support, so she was battling her demons alone. If she failed—if she went back to her old life—all that beauty and humor inside of her would suffocate and die. I couldn't let that happen.

"Because you can't," Link said, reading my expression like only he could. "I know you, brother. If you could have walked away, you and I wouldn't be having this conversation. You came here lookin' for a way out, thinkin' I'd tell you to respect her wishes and leave her alone. Which makes me wonder who the fuck you are, and what you've done with my brother."

He was pissing me off. "Come again?" I asked.

"You think Emily didn't tell me to leave her alone? You think she didn't fear this thing between us? I know I made it look easy, but I sure as hell didn't just waltz in there and tell her to marry me." He laughed. "It took work. And time. You're into this woman. You can fight your feelings all you want, but eventually you'll find yourself on her doorstep with no clue how you got there or what you're gonna say when she opens the door. Trust me. I couldn't have left Emily alone if my life depended on it. I hear the brothers talking about me like I'm pussy whipped. Wasp thinks I'm crazy for getting married so soon. But I don't give a single fuck, because that woman is my life. I would do anything for her. But I can't tell you what Julia is to you. You gotta figure out that shit for yourself. What I don't understand is why you haven't driven over there and talked to her. You know where she works and lives. What are you waiting for?"

"If she went back to him, I don't know how I'll react."

"Went back to him?" Link frowned. "The ex? Nothing you've said leads me to believe she'd do that. You gotta give her some credit."

"I'm not trying to end up in jail again, Link."

He shrugged. "If you do, maybe you'll find us another prospect. I like Stocks. He's a good man. Look for another like him, will ya?"

"I'm serious."

"Then don't do anything stupid. Control your fuckin' temper, Havoc. If she's back with him, she's not the woman you think she is and you need to walk the fuck away. Is that what you need to hear from me?"

Probably, but it still hurt like a motherfucker. I sucked down the last of my beer and leaned forward with my elbows on my knees. "Sometimes you're a real asshole, you know that?"

Chuckling, he spread his hands in surrender. "My most redeeming quality." Then, softening his tone, he added, "Look, she's been through a lot of shit. You both have. Maybe she's tryin' to figure out where you fit into her life. It's probably difficult for her to trust you... or anyone. It's gonna take work and time and you gotta figure out if she's worth all that." He scooted back up to his laptop, looking at the screen as his fingers landed on the keyboard.

"So, get the fuck out of my office and quit being such a damn pussy. And don't call me if your crazy ass ends up in jail over this."

It wasn't what I wanted to hear, but I needed to hear it. I liked Julia, and I needed to do something about it or shut the fuck up and move on.

"Fuck you, too," I said with a chuckle, standing. Link was just busting my balls. We both knew that he'd be my one call regardless of what I got arrested for. Just like we both knew he'd bail me out. Again.

He flipped me off as I walked out of his office.

12

Julia

TEN MINUTES TO closing time, and the store had been empty for almost an hour when the bell above the door rang. I glanced up from my novel to greet the last-minute book junkie, but froze at the sight of Wesley wearing a suit and a smug smile as he made a beeline for me. My body tensed, and I reached for my phone.

"You can't be here. I'm calling the cops."

"Again, with the dramatics? You know that restraining order didn't stick. I've only been staying away to give you time, Julia." He sighed and took another step toward me. "Oh, wait, you like to be called Jules now, don't you?"

My fingers froze on the keypad of my cell and my heart leapt into my throat as the douche canoe twisted the nickname that had made me feel warm and treasured into a shiv and shanked me right in the back. Only Havoc had ever called me Jules, and never where anyone could hear him. Now Wesley used it to cut deep, leaving me bleeding and exposed before him and facing the unthinkable. Still, I refused to believe it.

"Jules." He rolled the name around on his tongue, abusing and perverting it. "A bit immature for my tastes, but if you insist, I'll call you that."

"Please don't." I set my cell phone down as anger licked at my wounds, ready to cover the pain and protect me. I slipped on a mask and pretended to be unaffected by his presence or his knowledge. "In fact, don't call me anything. Ever again. Get out of my store, Wesley." I pointed to a sign over the cash register that declared I had the right to refuse service to anyone.

He stepped closer. "Why would you refuse *me* service when *he's* the one who betrayed you? It wasn't even difficult," he gloated. "I flashed him some cash and he rolled right over. He has bills to pay. I have deep pockets. You know the drill, Julia. You're the one who helped me perfect that particular tactic. Find their weakness, their currency. Isn't that what you always said to do?" He stepped around the counter to stand beside me. "Would you like to know what Havoc's currency is?"

Frozen, I watched him approach as I fought to wrestle my emotions under control. Yes, Wesley knew stuff he shouldn't know, but I was still having trouble believing Havoc would sell me out. I hung onto that thread of faith in his character while my training plucked away at it, reminding me that everyone has a price. Why should the biker be any different?

"I'm sure he didn't want to do it, but his mom needs an expensive operation... some tragic story about the valves of her heart or something. He's such a nice guy; he couldn't just let her die. Not when he had the opportunity to save her."

Oh God. That sounded like something Havoc would do. A deal he'd make with the devil. My knees felt weak and my chest tightened, making it impossible to breathe. Gripping the countertop, I refused to give Wesley the satisfaction of seeing me react. "What do you want from me?" I asked.

"Isn't it obvious?" he asked. "I want you back home. You belong to me, Julia. Jules. That fact didn't change because you needed a divorce and time, so you could deal with the consequences of your mistake. But as I told you back then, the only thing permanent is us. You have been mine since we were children, and I have been patient, but I'm ready for you to come back home and take your place at my side. I understand it will be an adjustment for you, so I'm prepared to make a few allowances. You can keep the bookstore. You won't be able to spend as much time here, of course, but you can staff it. Control it. I'll ignore the financial drain to make you happy."

"How very kind of you," I deadpanned as rage continued to stoke the fire inside me.

"What can I say? I'm a giver." Again with the smug smile. "If you insist on continuing this perverted affair with Havoc, I'll keep paying him to fuck you." His jaw twitched. "As long as you're discreet, of course. Wouldn't want people to talk, would we? I would like to watch, though. I do love to watch you get fucked."

The insinuation that he would have to pay someone—anyone—to fuck me was the last drop of gasoline my rage needed to become an inferno. "I would rather write a PhD dissertation about the cultural impact of queefs, complete with diagrams and a humiliating live demonstration, than live with you again."

His jaw tensed. "You don't have a choice my bride. Remember those pesky terms and conditions of your trust fund?"

My stomach sank, and bile tickled the back of my throat at the reminder of the many ropes my parents had created to control me over the years.

"I asked them not to press the issue," Wesley said, softening his tone. "But it's time now. I need you back with me. The business needs you back."

I felt the noose tightening around my throat, cutting off my oxygen. I couldn't breathe. Couldn't think. All I could do was rage. "Get out!" I shouted, scanning the area for something I could cut or shoot him with. Nothing. Dammit! My cell phone was the closest thing at hand, so I grabbed it and launched it at Wesley.

He ducked, and it shattered against the wall behind him before crashing to the hardwood floor. I didn't care. I grabbed pens and started pelting them at him. He swatted at them as he backed away.

"I see you require more time to accept your fate." He rounded the counter, putting it between us once again. "This is happening, Julia. We can do it the easy way, or the hard way, but my patience is coming to an end. If I don't hear from you by this weekend, I'll have to press the issue."

"How dare you!" I shouted. "You can't blackmail me into being with you!"

"Really?" he asked, shaking his head. "That's your defense? Pathetic. But don't worry, your mother will have you back to your old self in no time."

The paperback I'd been reading was the next thing I lobbed at him. He didn't bother ducking and as it bounced off his shoulder and hit the floor, he laughed. "I miss that fire. That passion. Don't let Havoc fuck that out of you before you come home. I'll see you this weekend," he said confidently before strolling out the door.

I looked for something else to throw, but there was nothing except my laptop and he was already gone. Angry, frustrated, ready to kill the mother-fucker for good, I regained hold of the countertop and seethed, throwing a toddler sized tantrum on the inside.

In the middle of my mental fit, Havoc appeared. He calmly reached behind him to close and lock the door before turning around the open sign and flicking the outside lights off. I stilled and watched him, raging inside as my heart and mind once again battled. Anger beat the shit out of both organs and poured itself into my index finger as I raised it and stabbed the air between us.

"You. You could have told me about your mom. I would have helped you. Why the hell would you go to *him*? Was it your manly pride that couldn't allow you to accept help from me?" I laughed, sounding manic and crazed, as tears of anger and helplessness flooded my eyes. Swallowing around the lump forming in my throat, I said, "You should leave."

"What are you talking about, Jules?"

"He fucking called me that!" I shouted. Tears leaked from my eyes. I swiped them away. "How could you? Why are you here? Did you come to gloat?" A sob ripped through me. "Because that cancerous cumstain beat you to it."

Havoc looked from me to the door. "I'm here because you're not returning my calls or texts. Other than the text telling me to leave you alone. Then I see that asswipe leaving and you're in here losing your shit in full-on crazy redheaded white-chick mode and I don't know what the fuck is going on."

"I didn't send you a text to leave me alone."

"Are you back with him?" Havoc asked.

"You'd like that, wouldn't you? Would he give you a bonus?"

"What the fuck are you talking about?"

Done screwing around, I shouted, "Did he pay you to fuck me?"

"What?" Havoc took a step toward me, hands out, stance non-threatening while anger ignited in his eyes. "Is that what you think? Why you told me to leave you alone?"

"I didn't. And he knows things, Havoc! Shit he has no business knowing. How the fuck did he know about your pledge to make me scream your name if *you* didn't tell him?"

"I don't know. I can't believe you think I'd tell that dipshit anything! What kind of man do you think I am?" Anger radiated off him, blending with mine. He grew darker, bigger, more dangerous.

Lightning crackled in the middle of my bookstore. I knew I should seek cover, but I was so far beyond self-preservation that I stepped closer and lent the storm my thunder.

"How the hell do I know? I know nothing about you. You showed up right when I needed a date and conveniently agreed to join me. Doesn't that sound a little suspect to you? I mean, why would you agree to go to a wedding with someone you don't even know?"

"Have you ever looked at yourself in the mirror?" His gaze landed on my lips before gobbling up the rest of my body. "You're a knockout, Jules. You could ask any man in this city and he'd take you anywhere you wanted to go. And if you weren't so busy trying to control every goddamn situation and emotion, and allowed yourself to be that vulnerable, gorgeous, real woman you showed me on the ferry, this thing between us could be amazing."

I blinked, trying to process his compliments as one ragged breath after the next ripped from my chest. He'd called me a knockout. Vulnerable. Gorgeous. Real.

"You know what I think?" he asked, storming on. "You know damn well what's going on, and you refuse to admit it because you'd rather blame me. It's safer. Easier. That way you don't have to feel anything. You're being a goddamn coward right now. Stop with the ice queen bullshit and admit you like me."

I wasn't a coward or an ice queen. My problem was the opposite. I wanted to go all in and feel all the things with Havoc. "Fuck you," I said.

He quirked an eyebrow at me and that cocky smirk reappeared, tinted with anger. It was hot. And irritating. I couldn't decide if I wanted to slap it or kiss it away.

"Is that an offer?" he asked, his gaze once again raking over my body.

No.

Yes.

No.

How dare he think he could stroll in here and fix everything by turning this to sex? I went to slap that cocky smirk right off his face, but he caught my hand. Looking into my eyes, he said, "You don't wanna do that, babe."

Yes, I did. I wanted to wail on him, and then kiss his wounds. It was sick and twisted, but I couldn't help it. I brought my other hand up, but he caught that one, too. As he held me captive, the hungry look he gave me sent a heatwave directly to my lady bits.

"Talk to me, babe," he said, his voice pleading.

"Your mom doesn't need heart surgery?"

"No. And if she did, I'd handle it. I already told you, I'm a man. I don't need a fuckin' handout. What the hell makes you think I'm so hard up I'd take anyone's money? Especially a little piss ant like Wesley's. Think about what you're accusing me of. It makes no sense. Had that dipshit so much as approached me with an offer, I'd be in jail right now."

Gazes locked, chests heaving, we stayed trapped in that moment as my mind unraveled Wesley's lies. Havoc hadn't betrayed me. Had done nothing to hurt me. He was still the incredible hero who swooped in and rescued me from soloing my sister's wedding. The realization sent more heat through my body. Obviously sensing the change in me, Havoc's eyes darted down to my lips. I ran my tongue across them. He released my hands and our bodies and mouths mashed together, fueled by some savage, primal need to recapture what we'd started after the wedding. To recapture what Wesley had tried to destroy.

Hands groping, desperate to get closer to him, my legs wrapped around his waist. My tight skirt rode up around my hips, no doubt showing my business to anyone who passed by the storefront windows, but I didn't care. Havoc hadn't sold me out to my evil ex. He was here, and I was no longer alone. The ache that had been eating away at my insides ebbed away, leaving only single-minded desire behind. Havoc pressed me against him as he deepened the kiss. He backed us both up, away from the view of passersby, and settled my back against a bookshelf. I broke away long enough to get my bearings. A loud rip caught my attention before my blouse fluttered down to land at my feet.

"You ripped my shirt!" I said, appalled even as my nipples strained against the fabric of my bra and more heat rushed to my core.

His hands squeezed my breasts, then reached around to free them. "You'll forgive me."

Yes, I would. As his thumbs flicked my taught nipples and his lips trailed down my neck, I wondered if there was anything I wouldn't forgive Havoc for. Especially now that I knew he wasn't a traitor.

"What do you want, Jules?" he asked before ducking to suck a nipple into his mouth.

"I want you to fuck me," I breathed.

"I will." His attention shifted to my other nipple. "But first, I need to taste your sweet pussy again."

Before I could argue, he lowered me to the floor and kneeled before me. There was another rip, and my panties joined my blouse as a sacrifice to his breathtaking passion. Havoc attacked my pussy like a starving man. There was nothing gentle about his barrage of licking and sucking as he grabbed my ass and pressed me against his mouth. I bounced off the bookshelf, loosening a handful of books. They wobbled on the edge, and the next time my back hit the shelf, they crashed to the floor. I should care about that, but he raked his teeth over my clit and I temporarily lost vision.

He spread me wider, exposing me. I rocked against his mouth as the indecency of it made me greedier for him. Harder and faster his tongue darted inside me, moving his hands to my hips to pull and push my body in sync with his attacks. More books fell, the sound of them tumbling to the ground registering somewhere in the back of my mind. I grabbed his head and pulled him into me as I shattered around his tongue.

He gave me only seconds to recover before I heard the rip of a condom package and his jeans hit the floor. Then my feet left the ground as he wrapped my legs around him again. He hefted my ass up, and then impaled me on his hard cock, stretching me to fit his impressive girth.

"Shit," he hissed. "You are so fucking tight."

138

Pumping me up and down his cock, he carried me to the overstuffed chair at the end of the aisle. He pulled out long enough to bend me over the back of the chair, so he could enter me from behind.

"Damn, I have missed this pussy," he said, groping my breasts. "And these tits. Fuck, Jules, you don't even know what you do to me. I want to do all kinds of nasty, fucked up shit to you."

"Prove it." I pushed against him. "Stop holding back."

He stilled, gripping my hips. "You don't know what you're asking for."

I giggled and looked at him over my shoulder. "You sure about that? Because I know the bitch inside me, and she wants to play with the beast in you. Let him free." I slammed my ass against the front of Havoc, taking him in deeper. "Free us both."

His nostrils flared, and his eyes darkened. He hiked my legs up over his hips and thrust into me, getting so damn deep he ripped a cry from my chest.

"You okay?" he asked.

"Dammit. Yes. Harder. More. Fuck me!"

Grabbing my thighs for leverage, he did exactly that. Each thrust was harder and deeper than the last, forcing me to brace against the chair. I welcomed the pounding, reveling in every plunge and grunt, feeling like he truly was setting me free. He kept it up until we heard a loud crack. One of the chair's wooden legs gave out, wobbling forward with Havoc's next thrust.

"Shit!" he exclaimed.

I laughed. "Don't stop. Things were just getting good."

"That sassy little mouth of yours will get you in trouble someday." He turned me to straddle him and moved us to the wall. Then to the floor. By the time we both found release, there were books everywhere, my chair was broken, and I had hardwood floor burn on my back (which I didn't even know was a thing), but I felt at peace for the first time in days.

Three days to be exact.

"Sorry about your chair," Havoc said, collapsing beside me and tucking me under his arm.

I giggled. "No, you're not."

He chuckled. "Yeah, you're right. I enjoy fuckin' you until we break the furniture. How about you? How do you feel? Better?"

I took a deep breath and blew it out. "Yeah. I've still gotta kill Wesley, but at least I can think to come up with a plan now."

"I think they call that pre-meditated, babe."

I didn't care, because now I knew what the lying little weasel had done. "He bugged my apartment. I have to figure out how and where."

Determined to put a stop to Wesley's snooping, I tried to get up, but Havoc wouldn't release me. "Let me handle that, babe. I have some brothers who worked in intelligence in the service. They'll sweep this entire place and make sure it's clean."

"You trust them?"

"With my life. And they know their shit. They'll be far more thorough than you and I would be."

"Thank you." I took another deep breath. "I'm sorry I didn't trust you, I just..."

"Shh." He pulled me against him and kissed my

forehead. "Trust is earned. You can't force that shit. I'll earn it, Jules. Or..." He flashed me that sexy smirk again. "I'll fuck you into submission while we break the rest of your furniture."

Cocky. I liked it. Kissing him on the chin, I said, "Promises, promises."

13

Havoc

MORSE AND TAP, two of my club brothers, arrived shortly after Julia and I cleaned up the mess we'd made of her bookstore. Except for the chair, since it would take a professional to fix the leg we'd broken. The guys pulled out their equipment and went right to work, finding ten hidden cameras between Julia's apartment and bookstore. With her arms wrapped around herself, she stared in horror at the pile on her kitchen table, swearing up a storm.

"You should call the authorities," Tap suggested. He'd been an intelligence officer in the Air Force and knew his way around most high-tech equipment. He plucked a dime-sized disk from the pile, studied it, then flipped it through his fingers. "This is some good shit. Newer tech. Expensive. Can't be too difficult to track back to the original purchase."

"It won't matter," Julia replied, her gaze still locked on the pile like she couldn't believe it and was waiting for it to sink in. "Even if Wesley was stupid enough to buy these himself, our families have ties with most of the judges in Seattle. No charges will stick."

I draped an arm over her shoulders and pulled her against me, trying to reassure her. "He'll slip up. Everyone does. We took down the Kinlans, remember?"

"With an overwhelming amount of evidence, an FBI team, and a ton of witnesses who were being sex trafficked. These are just cameras." She gestured at the pile and shuddered. "Just the creepy, disgusting, perverted, twisted way my ex has kept tabs on me. That's all. I still can't believe you found one in my bathroom. What kind of depraved degenerate wants to watch people use the toilet? This is... unfathomable. How did he even get in here? How many times has he been in my home? What else did he do while he was in here?" Her gaze finally left the pile of cameras to dart around the apartment as she transitioned from shock to freak out mode. "I need to call a locksmith and change the locks and bring in security. How did he get past the alarm?"

She was spiraling, and there was no way I could leave her here alone. Squeezing her against me to remind her of my presence, I kissed her forehead and said, "Go put on some jeans and boots and pack a bag. You're staying at my house tonight."

It was more of a demand than an invitation, and Julia's disobedient nature picked right up on it. She looked up at me with an argument on her lips, but relief in her eyes. She needed an excuse to give in, and I was more than willing to oblige.

"If I have to take a shot at this motherfucker, I'll

143

do a hell of a lot more than graze his ass. And your dad's not gonna do shit to keep me out of jail. Come with me, or I'm camping on your doorstep with a shotgun."

She met my gaze. "Someone will call the cops."

"Ask me how many fucks I give."

"Okay, I'll go. But only because I want to be the one who puts a bullet in his heart." With that, she spun around and walked out of the room.

"Damn," Tap said, watching her go. "I don't know whether to be turned on or terrified.

Julia was in a fresh shirt (after I ripped her last one off) and the tight skirt and heels she'd been wearing when I showed up. Nothing Tap needed to see, especially not with the way he homed in on her ass. I stepped in front of him, blocking his view. "Go with terrified. But not of her."

The side of his mouth turned up in a smirk as his gaze met mine. "You laying claim, brother? I don't see a property patch on her."

Which was going to be a problem when she helped us with the homeless outreach. I'd have to let the rest of the horny bastards know what was up, or I'd be busting faces the entire day. "And I don't see a death wish on you, so you better keep your hands and eyes off her."

"It's like that, huh?" he asked. "I come and save the day and don't even get to make a play on the hot chick?"

The idea of anyone making a play on Julia made my head want to explode. I crossed my arms and stared him down. "It's exactly like that."

He held his hands up in surrender. "All right, all

right. I get it, man. Chill the fuck out and stop giving me the death glare. That shit makes me nervous."

Giving Tap one last look, I turned my attention to Morse. "How you doing tracking that feed?"

Morse was the club's communications guru. He had connections all over the city and could hack into more systems than I knew existed. And he was far too shy and quiet to hit on Julia, and too smart to screw with me. He blew out a frustrated breath. "Whoever set this up is good. They know their shit. They're bouncing the feed off towers all over the world. I can pin it down, but it's gonna take some time."

"All right. I'm gonna get Julia out of here before she climbs the walls. Pack this shit up and take it with you to the station. Let me know when you find something."

"You got it, brother. Does she have a bag or something I can put the cameras in? I want to keep them separate from my shit."

I went into the kitchen and opened drawers until I found gallon-sized baggies. Tossing one to Morse, I instructed him and Tap to let themselves out before heading for Julia's room to see how she was coming along. I found her standing in her closet, her expression blank.

"Jules?" I asked, sliding in beside her and settling my hand on the small of her back. "You okay?"

She shook herself and reached out to grab a shirt. "I never thought..." She took a deep breath and slid the blouse from its hanger. "I underestimated Wesley and overestimated myself. The worst part about this whole situation is that I know I'm missing something, but I can't figure it out."

"Talk through it," I said. "Tell me what you have so far."

"I knew walking away from him was too easy. After all the measures our parents had gone through to get us together, I expected resistance. Now I find out that he never left me alone, after all. He was watching me the whole time." She shook her head and replaced the hanger. "And now he's suddenly going through extremes to get me back."

"Maybe he finally wised up and realized what he lost?" I suggested with a shrug.

She flashed me a grateful smile before shaking her head. "There must be more to it than that. He set up the bitch squad's betrayal. He wanted me to find out he was fucking my friends, or he wouldn't have propositioned Laura. It's like he wanted me to leave, but why? And my parents... they were so weird about our split. Almost like they didn't care, which is so *not* my mom. She controls every single detail, yet she let me run my own life for the past year. Now they want to repossess my freedom and force me back. Why now? What changed?"

The logic of people like Julia's parents was well beyond me, but I fully understood why the shithead wanted her back. One look at her in that bridesmaid dress had practically driven me over the edge, and that was before I got a taste of her sweet pussy. She wasn't the type of girl you let walk out of your life. Not even if she was pointing a rifle at you. "I know things are shit between you and your parents, but have you tried talking to them about this? Maybe they can shed some light on what's going on?"

"They'll only tell me what Wesley wants me to know. Their interests are in keeping the relationship with him and his parents strong, and keeping the business profitable. It would benefit them if I went back to him. In fact, they're going to cripple me unless I do."

"Cripple you how?"

"Financially. I blew through my savings on the purchase of the bookstore and furnishing my apartment, and the payments of my trust fund come with several conditions. My marriage to Wesley being the most onerous. My parents have let our divorce slide for the past year, but Wesley informed me that if I don't go back by the end of this weekend, they will cut me off immediately."

"What are you gonna do?"

"I don't know. I've made some solid investments, and they'll help me stay afloat for a while, but the bookstore is a drain. Without my trust fund payments... I'll have to do the math to make sure, but I think I'll only be able to keep it open five or six months. Maybe seven at the most."

They were taking away her options to force her hand, and she wasn't sure what she'd do. Fearing the answer, but needing clarification, I asked, "You're not thinking about going back to him?"

Disgust contorted her face. "To that rabid cuntroach? No thank you."

"Cuntroach?" I asked with a chuckle. Between the military and the motorcycle club, you'd think I'd heard all the insults known to man, but Julia's vocabulary never ceased to impress me.

"*Rabid* cuntroach," she corrected. "He lacks the balls of a cockroach, but he's diseased and delusional and forgets he's nothing but a pussy."

"Sounds like we need to figure out what bit him, then."

Her brows drew together as she studied me. "This isn't your fight, Havoc. You have gone above and beyond the call of duty. Even when I doubted you and thought you were working with the enemy. Wesley is powerful. With our parents backing him, he's virtually untouchable. There will be consequences for opposing him, and I don't want you caught up in that. You're a good guy, and you don't deserve any of this."

She looked so fragile and on edge I needed to touch her, to hold her together so she wouldn't shatter. I reached out and cradled her face in my hand, our gazes still locked. "You're a friend, Jules, and I don't give that title away lightly. I have your back, and I told you, I fight dirty. I have no intention of letting this rabid cuntroach win."

Her expression softened, and her shoulders relaxed. She dropped the blouse she'd been holding as my hand slid through her hair and I grabbed the back of her head, pulling her against me for a kiss. She didn't resist, and before I knew it, I had her pressed against the closet wall with my hand up her skirt, pleased to find that she hadn't replaced the panties I'd ripped off. Julia's ability to make me lose control was staggering. I'd never met someone so irresistible. Yes, I'd have her back, but my motives were more selfish than I'd let on. I didn't want to lose her—to lose this connection between us—and I'd fight any motherfucker to keep it. To keep her, I would fight as dirty as necessary.

Julia's greedy pussy squeezed around my fingers as I continued to kiss her gently. She still seemed so damn fragile that I wanted to comfort and protect her rather than fuck her senseless. The desire was new to me, but not unwelcome. Keeping my lips on hers, I scooped her up, cradling her in my arms, and took her to her bed. Lying her down, my kisses roamed down her neck to explore her body, but she stopped me, pulling my face back up to hers.

"I need you inside me now," she pleaded.

I grabbed a condom from my pocket and dropped my pants.

Her gaze drifted to the packet in my hand, and she shook her head. "I'm clean and on the pill. I need to feel *you* inside me."

She didn't even ask if I was clean, and that spoke volumes about how much she trusted me. I'd never been inside a woman without a glove. Not once. I didn't screw around with that shit. Yet the need and vulnerability written across Julia's face made me drop the condom beside my pants. As I climbed on top of her, my lips found hers again. I lifted her skirt and used the tip of my cock to tease her clit.

"Please?" she asked.

Unable to deny her, I positioned myself at her entrance and slid in. Holy shit! Her pussy felt like silk as it wrapped around me, so tight and perfect. She let out a gasp and hooked her legs behind my back, taking me in deeper. I couldn't even remember the last time I'd fucked a girl missionary style, but as Julia drew comfort from my lips and my cock, I couldn't bear to break the connection. Something between us seemed to shift, to deepen as I slowly slid in and out of her while our tongues danced. We weren't fucking. This was different. More. Something I'd never experienced. There was no desperate frenzy to find release, because neither of us wanted it to end.

Her hands drifted up my shirt, rubbing over my muscles before exploring my back and drifting down to squeeze my ass. Content to let her play, I braced myself on my forearms on either side of her head and continued to explore her mouth as I slowly slid in and out of her. We kept it up for a while before neither of us could hold back anymore. I grabbed her ankles and rested them on my shoulders, getting impossibly deeper. She threw back her head and moaned. The sexy sound encouraged me, and I plowed into her until we both found release.

After we finished, I moved to roll off her, but she wrapped her legs around me, keeping me still and inside her. "Please, just stay here a minute more."

Her eyes were watering.

The sight made my chest tighten. "Hey, it'll be all right, Jules," I said, smoothing her hair away from her face. With her hair mussed and her cheeks flushed, she was radiant. Even as a tear rolled down her cheek.

She closed her eyes, releasing more tears. She ducked her head against my chest and I wrapped my arms around her, holding her as she sobbed. It made me want to find this Wesley fucktard and beat the shit out of him. But Julia needed me present, so I pushed thoughts of her ex away. Keeping us connected, I rolled over until she was on top of me. Then I patted her back and brushed her hair out of her face, encouraging her to take all the time she needed.

Eventually her tears dried up. She pushed off my chest and released my cock to sit up, her cheeks pink with embarrassment. "Sorry. I made a mess of your shirt."

Shrugging, I sat up and snaked an arm over her shoulders, unable to keep my hands off her. "It's okay, babe. We're going to my house and I can change. You need to get some jeans and boots on, though." I squeezed her thigh. "We're taking my bike, and I don't want anything to happen to these perfect legs."

Giving me a shy smile, she said, "Thanks. For everything. I don't know what I'd do without you."

Needing to lighten the mood, I replied, "Of course. Anytime you need to punch that benefit card, all you have to do is ask. I'll be more than happy to put it on you."

Rolling her eyes, she gave me a little shove before standing to go clean up and get dressed. I got myself together and watched as she packed a bag, strangely excited about taking her home.

14

Julia

SITTING ON HAVOC'S bed, I stared into the mirror above his chest of drawers and gave myself a little a pep talk to prepare for the day. In less than ten minutes, Havoc and I would leave for his club. There, I'd meet all the guys he referred to as brothers and I'd wait on homeless people. No big deal. Only it was. It would be my first social gathering since Laura's wedding, and I honestly didn't want to people anymore. Possibly ever again. In fact, if I could just go back to my bookstore and read for the rest of my life, I'd be perfectly happy.

Well... as long as Havoc dropped by daily to rock my world.

That line of thinking started me down a bunny hole as I thought of how we'd christened every room of his house. I say christened, because apparently, he'd never brought a woman home before.

I laughed when he told me, figuring it was a joke. Only he didn't join in.

"*You're saying you don't have sex?*" *I asked, eyeing him skeptically. We were in the laundry room, where we'd just discovered that the washing machine was the perfect height for me to sit while Havoc fucked me, which only improved when the spin cycle starting in the middle of the act. We'd gotten our rocks off, and the washer had stopped. Now, I was sitting on it and folding shirts while Havoc paired socks and folded pants.*

"*Nope. Didn't say that at all. I have a room at the club I take broads to.*"

"*Is this like some kinky sex club?*" *I asked.*

He shook his head. "*Nope. Well... define kinky. Some guys and club whores like to fuck in public. They get off on that sort of thing.*"

"*Do you?*" *I asked.*

"*The idea appeals to me, but I told you, I don't share. When you do shit like that in public, people think they can join in. Any motherfucker who lays a finger on what's mine will end up in the hospital.*"

"*Yours, huh?*" *I arched an eyebrow.* "*Possessive much?*"

"*Like a fuckin' treasure-hording dragon.*" *Giving me a heated look, he added,* "*Jules.*"

The insinuation that I was his jewel activated a whole new set of warm and fuzzy feelings inside me. My cheeks heated as I grabbed one of my dresses out of the dryer.

"*What about you?*" *he asked.* "*You like the idea of getting fucked in public?*"

I wanted to deny it, but the wanton little bitch inside of me provided several scenarios that made me wet. "*That could be fun,*" *I replied.* "*I wouldn't want anyone to join in, either. I wouldn't want anyone to even know.*"

"Stealthy public sex?" he asked, sliding his fingers up the inside of my thigh. "That has potential. I'll see what I can do." Before I could tell him that wasn't necessary, his fingers paused at the hem of my shirt—a T-shirt I'd stolen from his drawer—and he leaned in and kissed me softly. "Like you in my clothes, babe."

I smiled against his lips. "Is that why you rip off anything else I put on?"

"I told you, my house has rules. No bras, no panties, no pants."

"And yet, you just admitted that I'm the first woman you've ever brought here. Sure you're not making this up as you go?"

He shrugged, and his fingers resumed their track up my thigh. Circling my clit, he kissed me through my gasp. "You don't seem to mind. You're soaked, babe. Again."

I couldn't help it. He'd turned me into some sort of insatiable sex fiend and I wanted him inside me all the time. "Are you complaining?" I fired back.

He wrapped my legs around him and grabbed my ass. "Fuck no. I say we hit the garage next."

"You almost ready?" Havoc asked, interrupting my flashback.

Blowing out a breath, I stood and gave myself one last look. Havoc had picked me up a Harley Davidson T-shirt and requested that I wear it with jeans and boots for two reasons. So we could ride his bike, and because the rest of my clothes were far too sexy, and he didn't want to have to kill one of his brothers. I'd gone light on the makeup and blown my hair out into big curls that would no doubt get wrecked during the ride.

"You look great," he said, hooking his thumbs into my waistband and pulling me to him. "They're gonna love you. Which is exactly what I'm worried about."

My worries leaned more toward discovering their weaknesses and involuntarily using them to blackmail everyone into pretending like they liked me, since that was more my thing. Making friends authentically... not so much.

When we arrived at the old fire station that served as the club's base of operations, Havoc started behaving strangely. He helped me off his bike, removed my helmet, and then tucked me securely under his arm. We entered what he referred to as "the common area" as one, and as he introduced me to his brothers and their significant others, he kept me tight against him. A dark-haired, tall, wiry man walked in with his arms full of giant condiment containers and I tried to break free to help him, but Havoc held me back.

"What are you doing?" I asked, irritated. "I thought you brought me here to help, not to be your arm candy. Aren't we supposed to be doing something?"

His expression drew tight as he scooted me out of the hustle and bustle and released me beside the wall. "Yes. Just be careful."

"What do you mean, be careful?" I turned to face him. "These are your brothers, right? What are you worried about?"

His hand cupped my cheek, and his gaze locked on mine. "You have no idea how beautiful you are, Jules, and there are some horny motherfuckers up in this place. I don't want to bury any of my brothers, and the way some of them are lookin' at you is already makin' my blood boil."

He was jealous, and it was hot. The passion and fervor in all Havoc's emotions seemed to turn me on. He felt things so deeply and unlike me, he wasn't afraid to let his emotions show.

But then he had to ruin it by adding, "Bringing you here was a mistake."

Irritated that he would rather keep me from people who were such a big part of his life than deal with his jealousy, I asked. "Then why did you make this a condition to our original deal?"

Studying me, he frowned. "Because you need it. Serving others will help you uncover the good inside you. Help you see that not everything you do is self-serving." His thumb gently ran across my lower lip. "You've done some fucked up shit and now you think you're some kind of monster, but you've never had the chance to be anything else. Doing shit for people who can't do anything for you is... it helps me control the beast. I'm betting it's what you need, too."

He was such a good man. I could serve others for the rest of my life and not be worthy of him. Raising up on my tiptoes, I planted a chaste kiss on his lips before pulling away. "Sounds like you need to put on your big boy panties and deal with your jealousy issues, so I can give my inner bitch a run for her money."

He chuckled. "Yeah, okay. But my jealousy issues make you wet."

"What?" I asked, heat racing to my cheeks.

"Don't deny it, Jules." Hooking his thumbs in the waistband of my jeans, he pulled me against him. "I can see it in your eyes. They darken. Your breath grows shallow. Babe, you have so many goddamn tells and they all make me want to bend you over one of these pool tables and fuck you."

A shiver went up my spine and more heat pooled between my legs. I pushed him away. "Stop that. Let me get to work. I'm sure there's something you should be doing."

"Havoc, Link's looking for you. He's out at the grill with Wasp and Eagle."

I turned toward the voice to find a familiar brunette watching us with an amused expression. Dressed in her own Harley Davidson T-shirt, jeans, and riding boots, Emily Stafford was also wearing a vest like Havoc's.

Surprise flickered across her expression as she focused on me. "Julia, right? Julia Benson?"

She remembered me. Dread clenched my stomach. "Julia Edwards. I went back to my maiden name."

"That's right. I recall your parents now." Her expression soured. "You probably don't remember, but I met you once. At the Seattle Children's Hospital Dinner, but you were..."

"A pretentious bitch?" I offered.

Her eyes widened in surprise, and then lit up and she snickered. "I was going to say still married, but your assessment is accurate as well."

Her honesty, paired with the knowledge of her taking down the Kinlans, endeared me to her instantly. "Sorry about that, Ms. Stafford. I assure you I have surgically removed the stick from my ass and am here to assist and hopefully atone for my sins."

"Emily," she corrected. "And you've come to the right place. The Dead Presidents know all about helping people find redemption. But I'm more curious about how this happened." Her gesture encompassed me and Havoc before she turned her attention on him. "Link needs your help. I'll watch out for her. She'll be fine."

"Thanks, Em," he said before giving me one last hug. "You need me, text me. I'll keep my phone on."

"Go. I can handle myself."

He took off and Emily's amused expression returned as she watched him leave. Turning toward me, she said, "I guess it's true... the bigger they are, the harder they fall."

Giggling, I felt some of the tension I'd been holding onto roll off my shoulders as I followed Emily into the dining area. The back of her vest had the same Dead Presidents MC logo as Havoc's, but hers also had two extra patches at the bottom that labeled her as "Property of Link." Confused, I asked, "Did they make you an honorary biker or something for helping with Havoc's case?"

"No." She laughed. "This bunch of knuckle-draggers wouldn't allow a woman to join their club. I'm engaged to Link, the club president, and he gave me this cut to wear at club functions. It reminds his men that I belong to him, so he doesn't have to beat on his chest and chase them away."

And if Link was anything like Havoc, I could picture that happening. "Primitive," I replied.

More laughing. "You have no idea."

"But property of...?" I asked. "Don't you find that demeaning?"

She shook her head. "I thought I would, but there's something to be said for a man who's not afraid to throw you over his shoulder and carry you to his hut. But by the way Havoc was looking at you, I'm guessing you understand that firsthand. How'd you two meet?"

"He needed to keep his flowers alive; I needed a date for my sister's wedding. We worked out an exchange."

Emily spun around and studied me, her eyes bright and a smile spread across her face. "*You* own that little bookstore downtown?"

I nodded.

"I sent him there. Gardening was supposed to chill him out, but it appears he found something else to do the trick." She shook her head. "I can't imagine him voluntarily attending a wedding of Seattle's elite. Hell, I can't imagine him being forced into it. He wore a suit?"

"Yep, and he looked delicious."

"Hm. That settles it. Link and his groomsmen are wearing suits. I was on the fence—considering keeping the dress casual—but if Havoc survived, Link will, too. Although I do like him in nothing but jeans..."

I looked around the station, taking in all the good-looking bikers. "That might be a bit too casual. This group, bare chested, could cause mass swooning."

Emily's smile widened. "It's nice to have you here, Julia. I sure am glad you had that surgery."

Feeling welcome, I smiled and thanked her as we started arranging condiments on the tables and organized serving stations. Emily introduced me to the old ladies and club whores. Havoc had explained the titles to me this morning, but the way the women embraced those titles seemed strange to me. I still couldn't get over a strong independent woman like Emily wearing a property patch, but I really couldn't understand the club whores. Before I could ask her more about them, her grandmother and assistant showed up.

"Grandma, Jayson, this is Julia. She came with Havoc," Emily introduced us.

"You snagged big, dark, and handsome?" Jayson asked, getting right to work on the napkins and silverware. "Girl, I need details. Please tell me he is that big everywhere."

"Jay," Emily warned.

"Don't act like you're not curious," he replied before turning back to me. "So, what are we dealing with? It's bigger than a banana isn't it?"

The visual created by his examples made me laugh, but I needed to set Jayson straight. "We're not really *together*."

"But you have seen the D. Be honest, girl. I can tell you have by that look on your face. When you wrap your hand around it, does your finger touch your thumb?"

He was relentless. Giggling, I replied, "I'll measure him and get back to you."

Jayson's eyes widened comically. "Pictures, or it didn't happen."

"Jayson!" Emily snapped.

"What?" he shrugged, the picture of innocence. "Not everyone is stingy like you. Some people like sharing their dick pics. I know if I ever snag myself one of these big, hot bikers, I'm showing his equipment off to all of you."

Emily rubbed her temple. "Please, for the love of all that is holy, do not send me dick pics. Of anyone."

He rolled his eyes. "You're such a killjoy."

They were ridiculous, and their antics helped me relax even more as I joined Jayson in laying out the silverware. As I finished up my second table, a group of bikers walked in carrying boxes toward the kitchen. I felt a couple of them give me the once over, but a man with a shaved head and a bit of a beer belly was leering with an intensity that made me uncomfortable. Trying to ignore him, I grabbed a stack of glasses and began setting them out.

He stopped beside me and said, "Hey, baby. You must be new here. After the dinner, you wanna go up to my room and watch porn on my flat screen mirror?"

That was the most pathetic line I'd ever heard. Shocked that anyone would be so forward and crude, I looked up from the glasses in time to catch his gaze raking over my body. "Uh... hard pass, but thanks. I think." I kept my tone polite, but my words came out clipped.

"Come on, babe. Your pussy's not any better than any other club whore's. It'll get passed around and land in my bed sooner or later."

"Buddha," Emily said, wedging her way between us. "Julia is not a club whore. She came with Havoc."

161

He eyed me. "I don't see no property patch."

Emily put her hands on her hips. "I suggest you take that up with Havoc, then. But remember that lots of volunteers are here helping today, so if you could kindly refrain from hitting on them and making them uncomfortable, I'd appreciate it."

He looked like he was about to argue, but one of the other bikers called his name and leveled a glare at him. Looking over Emily's shoulder at me, Buddha said, "I'll see you around," before he took off.

Emily let out a breath, whispering, "Douchebag."

The biker who'd been staring down Buddha joined us, asking, "Everything all right, Em?"

She nodded, smiling at him. "It is now. Thanks Bull. This is Julia. She's with Havoc."

Bull shook my hand. He was young, maybe in his early twenties, tall, good looking, with a smile that didn't quite reach his eyes. "Nice to meet you, ma'am," he said, with a slight southern drawl. "Havoc's a good man. You need anything, you let me know."

"Thanks. I'm not really *with* Havoc, though. We're just friends."

"Right," Emily said, giggling. "Good luck with that."

Bull stayed close to us for the rest of the setup, helping.

"Shouldn't he be with the other bikers?" I asked.

"He's a prospect. That's their rank before they become patched members. He's pretty much my bodyguard for all intents and purposes. Has Havoc 'put a man on you' yet?"

"You mean like saddling me with a bodyguard?" I asked. "No thanks. I'm good."

"Yep. It'll happen eventually. Probably about the time he shreds that friend card you're carrying around. Know that in your heart."

The idea of Havoc wanting more than friendship filled me with both dread and longing. Choosing to ignore both feelings, I went for a subject change. "Well, having a bodyguard isn't too bad. At least he got here before Buddha started humping my leg."

She laughed. "Buddha's not my favorite. Watch out for him. I just hope he's smart enough not to push anything. Havoc will lose his shit. Julia, I can tell you're uncomfortable with the topic, but you need to know that Havoc doesn't look at anyone the way he looks at you. Be careful with that one. He's a good man."

As we finished setting the tables, I let Emily's warning sink in, admitting the truth of it. I wasn't ready for another relationship, but I wasn't ready to let Havoc go, either. Hoping she was wrong, and he'd be content to stay friends for a while, I pushed the thoughts to the back of my mind and focused on welcoming the homeless guests as they entered and found seats.

15

Havoc

DESPITE MY CONCERNS about keeping my horny ass brothers away from Julia, dinner went off without a hitch. Emily stayed close to Julia, and Bull stayed close to Emily, scowling at anyone who got too close to the ladies. With Bull playing guard dog, I was free to do my job and stop worrying like some goddamn mother hen. I had no clue what the fuck was wrong with me. I'd always been protective of my friends, but with Julia it was different. Not only did I want to protect her, I wanted to stash her sexy ass away so only I had access to her. It was unrealistic and unreasonable, but I knew I'd found a gem and I didn't want any other motherfuckers to see her shine and get any ideas about taking her for themselves.

The guys and I found three promising veterans during dinner, which we would vet and assign to sponsors over the next few days. We cleaned up, and then the dozen of us who stayed late stuffed a cooler full of beer and carried it out back to gather around the fire pit and shoot the shit. Eagle and I got the fire going while the prospects brought out chairs for everyone. Keeping one eye on Julia, I chopped kindling as Eagle wadded up newspapers and tossed them into the pit.

"Julia, right?" Link asked, offering her his hand as he approached. "I'm Link. It's good to meet you. Sorry I didn't get around to introducing myself earlier, but I really appreciate you helping today."

"Don't even worry about it," she said, shaking his hand. "You looked a tad busy."

"Yeah, these dinners are a shit-ton of work. Worth it, though. What'd you think of it all?" he asked, tucking Emily under his arm.

"It was a lot... different than I imagined. The people were nice and grateful, but there were so many kids." She swallowed and took a moment before continuing, "I wasn't expecting that."

"Yeah, that shit's rough." He opened the cooler and started grabbing beers, passing them around the growing circle. He angled one toward Julia, but she declined. "It's easy to forget how big and fucked up the problem is until we invite them in and get to know them as people. Everyone's got a story, and their situations are enough to rip your goddamn heart out. I wish we could help them all, but our resources are limited, and our brothers are our priority."

A recruit offered Link a chair, and he sat, tugging Emily onto his lap.

"Family is everything," he said, rubbing her back

as she wrapped her arms around his neck. He kissed her forehead before claiming her lips.

Julia turned away from their public display of affection and rubbed her hands together before holding them out toward the growing fire. Wasp and I tented enough wood together in the pit to catch the flames from the kindling and I returned to Julia as Stocks offered her a chair. I introduced the two of them before stealing the chair and patting my lap.

She hesitated, glancing around, her stiff upbringing no doubt kicking in.

"It's getting cold," I said, offering a valid excuse. The temperature had dropped at least twenty degrees after the sun went down. June in western Washington was unpredictable at best. We were just lucky it wasn't raining. Wearing only a thin jacket over her T-shirt, she had to be chilly.

Accepting the excuse, she slid onto my lap, sitting sideways, and sought warmth by sliding her arms between my T-shirt and cut. Her proximity immediately began siphoning the day's stress and tension from my shoulders and encouraging most of my body to relax. Most of my body, because my dick hardened the second her fine ass hit my lap. I took a long pull from my beer and tried to focus on the surrounding conversation rather than the way her body curved around mine.

"Did you tell Julia what I found out?" Morse asked, sliding a chair beside us.

Julia perked up. "Tell me what?"

I hadn't told her shit, because I was concerned about how she'd react. I scowled at Morse, warning him to keep his trap shut, but his focus was on the electronic tablet in his hands.

"I followed the feeds from the cameras hidden in your apartment, and they all have something in common. They ping here." He showed her his screen. "It's a warehouse in the industrial district."

Emily sat up as well. "Someone hid cameras in your apartment?" she asked.

"My ex," Julia explained. "He's... uh..."

"Creepy?" Emily provided. "Stalkerish? Perverted?"

"All the above." Julia pointed at the screen. "That looks familiar. What's the address?"

Morse rambled off the address and asked, "Recognize it?"

"I think so." She pulled out her phone and thumbed it on, scrolling through her pictures. "Weird. It's not here. I transferred all my photos from my old SD card when I switched phones Thursday, but I don't see it. I'll have to go online to look, but I'm pretty sure this is where Wesley took the strippers."

My stomach sank. "What strippers?"

"Before we split up, he started acting weird, like he was hiding something from me. So, I went through his briefcase while he was asleep. I found a strange note... descriptions of some girls and an address. I Googled the address, and I'm almost certain this is the same warehouse the search led me to. Anyway, the descriptions of the girls were graphic. Explicit. Measurements, piercings, tattoos, whether they were bald, had a bush, or sporting a landing strip. That sort of thing. Disgusted, I snapped a picture of the note. Then I flipped out and confronted Wesley. He blew up about me going through his shit. Seriously, he went crazy. I'd never seen him so pissed. When he finally calmed down, he explained he was hiring strippers for some out-of-town businessmen. That made sense, but at the time, I didn't understand why it pissed him off so much. Now, I know he was probably hiring hookers for himself. Cheating whoreson."

The entire circle was staring at her as she confirmed what I'd suspected for the past two days.

"What?" she asked, her gaze flickering around the group before landing on me. Her body stiffened as she leaned away. "What's going on? Why do I feel like I'm missing something?"

I had no choice but to tell her. "That's one of the Kinlan warehouses, Jules."

Her face went through a series of emotions: thought, realization, shock, anger, disbelief. Finally, she shook herself and said, "Sex trafficking. That was one of the charges. You think...?"

I nodded.

She leapt off my lap and paced the space between Link and Emily's chair and mine. "You think Wesley was involved in sex trafficking."

"I'm so sorry, Julia," Emily said.

"But the FBI seized those warehouses. How would the signal still be pinging there or whatever?"

"It's not exactly in the building," Morse explained. "The city has a small satellite dish attached to the roof."

Julia stopped pacing and cradled her head in her hands. "That son-of-a-bitch. That son-of-a-disease-infested-maggot-ridden-whore was sex trafficking. Of all the depraved, messed up shit he could have possibly been doing. No wonder he pushed me away. I was asking questions, and he knew I'd find out, eventually. I always did." She wrapped her hands around her stomach. "That's what they trained me for. But, this is too much. I wouldn't have stood aside and let him do this shit. He knew, so he fucked around on me, making sure I found out and left. I always wondered why my parents didn't force me to go back to him. Why they continued to allow my payments even though I'd broken the terms. Either they knew what he was doing, or Wesley had told them it was okay." She shook her head.

Emily jumped to her feet and rubbed Julia's back.

"Mom had to know. She's like me, and she wouldn't have let it go. She fucking trained me."

I watched Julia shove the pieces together, wondering what to do. Emily looked helpless as she continued to pat her back.

"Now that it's all over and the Kinlans have been dealt with, Wesley needs me back so he can monitor me." She ran her hands through her hair and cradled the back of her neck, looking up at the sky. "Fuck! That's why he planted those cameras. Here I thought he was just a pervert, but no. He's been watching me this whole time to make sure I didn't put two and two together."

"You said you have the picture online?" Emily asked.

"I should. All my photos are supposed to be saved."

I had a bad feeling about where this was all going, so I stood and grabbed Julia's shoulders, forcing her attention onto me. "Are you sure you want to go down this road? The Kinlans died over this shit. What's stopping this asshole from coming after you?"

"He's already coming after me." She pulled up the messaging app on her phone and passed it to me. There were several texts from an unknown sender asking her where she was, what she was doing, and when she was coming back. Reminding her she only had until the end of the weekend.

"Why didn't you tell me?" I asked.

"My ex is not your problem. I already told him we aren't getting back together. It's not like he can force me to change my mind." She turned to Link and asked, "Is there a computer I can use to check my online storage?"

Link glanced at me.

Knowing Julia wouldn't be deterred, I nodded.

Soon, Link, Emily, Julia, Wasp, Eagle, Morse, Tap, and I were all huddled around Link's computer, staring at Julia's photos.

"It's not here," she said, sounding devastated. "I shouldn't be surprised, but I am. He must have hacked my account and deleted it."

I, for one, was relieved. "Sounds like there's nothing more you can do."

She didn't look so convinced, but she let me lead her back out to the fire pit.

"I feel so stupid," she said, climbing back on my lap. "I should have looked into it, but everything fell apart after that."

I'd been trying to tamp down my temper, but the entire situation was screwing with my mind. Wesley was dangerous, and she didn't seem to realize that. Afraid of her getting too ballsy and doing something stupid, I squeezed her against me, reassuring myself that she was okay. "I'm glad you didn't pursue it. Jules. We all know the Kinlans didn't hang themselves in some sort of father-son suicide pact. They aren't the type to go out like that. Emily said they were trying to cut a deal."

"I know," she admitted.

Yet, she didn't sound scared. "You're not bulletproof."

"I know."

Still not scared. "You can be poisoned, strangled, stabbed, suffocated, have your pretty little neck snapped, and he wouldn't have to do any of it. He could send someone to take care of his dirty work for him. Someone could walk right in your store, pull out a gun, and put a slug in you before you even knew what was happening."

She shuddered. "I know." This time her voice was shaky. Good. She needed to understand the severity of the situation.

"If he doesn't leave you alone, I'm gonna lose my shit and kill him."

"I know."

"Morse, tomorrow morning, will you have time to set a couple of those cameras back up in Julia's bookstore?" I asked.

Julia's brow furrowed. "You want to put them back up? Why?"

"We'll monitor the feed. Make sure he doesn't

try anything while you're working. Also, I'm putting a man on you."

Her gaze snapped to mine. "Who?"

Something about her tone and reaction set me on edge. "Probably Stocks, why?"

Her gaze fell to my chest. "No reason."

"We said no lies, Jules. What happened?"

She snuggled closer to me, splaying her hand across my chest. "Please, just let it go."

"Emily?" I asked, shifting my attention to her. "Did something happen today that I need to know about?"

The girls shared a look, and I got the feeling neither of them would tell me shit. Thankfully, they didn't have to, because Bull stepped in. "Buddha was hitting on her. Emily told him Julia was with you, but it didn't stop him. He wouldn't leave her alone until I stepped in. A couple of the other guys heard him, too."

"Motherfucker." I couldn't do a damn thing about Wesley right now, but Buddha hitting on my woman? That was something I *could* handle. I sprang to my feet, setting Julia down.

"Stop," she said, stepping in front of me. "He's your brother. Don't do something you'll regret."

The look I gave her should have made her cower in fear, but Julia's eyes darkened with lust instead. If I wasn't so pissed, I'd carry her ass upstairs and fuck that out of her, but Buddha had disrespected me, and I couldn't let that shit slide. Sidestepping her, I headed for the back door.

"Isn't anyone going to stop him?" Julia asked, sounding frantic.

"Nope," Link said, standing. "Wasp and I will follow him and make sure he doesn't take shit too far, but this is between the two of them. Buddha should have backed off the second Emily told him to, but if he thinks he's man enough to take on Havoc... who are we to stop him?"

"Buddha needs to be taught a lesson," Wasp added.

I couldn't hear anything else, because blood was rushing to my eardrums as I entered the station and headed upstairs to Buddha's room. I didn't bother to knock, and he hadn't bothered to lock his door, so I got an eyeful of a club whore named Kim going down on him as I stormed into the room. The door slammed against the wall, getting his attention.

"What the fuck, man?" Buddha asked over his shoulder.

"Kim, find somewhere else to be," I growled.

She released his cock and stood, squeezing past me to scurry out the door.

Buddha tucked himself back into his pants and zipped up, backing away from me. "I didn't know the broad was yours, Havoc. She wasn't wearing a property patch."

His lies were making the edges of my vision blur. Did he think I was stupid? That none of my brothers had my back enough to tell me what happened? I stepped forward, ready to lunge for him. If he thought he'd get away and run like a pussy, he had another think coming. "Bullshit. Emily told you what was up and you kept talking, disrespecting me in front of my woman and my club. You think I'm gonna let that shit slide?"

He took another step back, his hands raising as his gaze scanned the room. The motherfucker was looking for a weapon. Sure enough, he reached for some sort of trophy on the top of his dresser. I sprang forward, tackling him as he grabbed it. He swung at my head and I blocked, taking a hit across my forearm. Blood pounded in my ears and my vision went red. I ripped the trophy from his hand and threw it across the room before nailing him with an uppercut to the jaw. His head fell back, smacking against the hardwood floor as he brought his hands up to protect his face. Fine with me. Buddha had a nice round beer gut that made a perfect target. I punched him in the side, gaining a grunt before he recovered and tried to take a swing at me.

"You wanna hit me?" I asked, standing and gesturing him forward. "Get your ass up and do it."

His expression wary, he stood, raised his hands, and hopped around like we were about to box. I welcomed it, wanting a fight. A challenge. I didn't want to beat the shit out of him; I wanted us both bloody. He wanted Julia. Wesley wanted Julia. I needed someone I could sink my fists into. I didn't want to give in to battle rage. Wanting instead to remember every single swing, so I could feel like I'd earned her, but the bastard wouldn't stop bouncing around.

"Fuckin' hit me, you pussy!" I shouted.

He struck with a left hook. It barely grazed my chest as I stepped back.

"That all you got?" I asked.

His face was red. Good. I wanted him angry.

"What's wrong?" I took a jab at his face, but he

blocked me. "Can't find your own woman?" Another jab. He easily swatted it away. "Don't you have any balls, Buddha?"

He barreled into me, swinging wildly. The bastard nailed me in the ribs, and I returned the favor. His fist flew at my face, but I leaned out of reach and checked his shoulder. The motherfucker tried to swipe my legs out from under me. Steadying myself, I landed another right hook to his jaw. He wobbled back and forth, and then crumbled. The asswipe was out like a light, and it pissed me off because I still had a lot of rage to work out.

"Get up!" I shouted. "Get the fuck up and fight me!"

"He's done," Link said, stepping into the room and kneeling to check on Buddha. "And he's gonna have one hell of a headache."

"Yeah, well I'm not done."

Wasp joined Link. "Time to chill the fuck out, Havoc. Get out of here."

I was about to argue that I hadn't extracted the pound of flesh Buddha owed me, but Link stood beside Wasp, crossing his arms. Knowing neither of them would budge, I turned and stormed out.

16

Julia

"HOW LONG DOES this kind of thing usually last?" I asked Emily as I sipped the rum and diet soda she'd made me.

She shrugged. "Until the testosterone wears off or one of them needs stitches. Don't worry about Havoc, though. He can handle his own."

I definitely wasn't worried about Havoc.

"You two still mad at me?" Bull asked, popping the top off a beer and settling on the stool beside me.

Emily seemed to consider the question before answering. "No. If you had said nothing, Buddha probably would have kept it up and then Havoc would have done much worse. You may have just saved a life, Bull."

"Hey, that's what I do," he said with a shrug. He tapped me on the shoulder. "Don't worry about him. The big guy's gonna be just fine."

Worrying hadn't even crossed my mind. After

seeing Havoc in all his jealous fury, I was so damn horny I could hardly think straight, much less worry. I wanted his energy. All that delicious emotion should be fucking me, not getting wasted on a fight with Buddha. I had to be the most fucked up person on the planet. Fully aware that Havoc's rage should have me running in the opposite direction, not fantasizing about putting him in a headlock with my legs, I struggled to get myself under control. He was a bull, pawing at the ground and preparing to charge, and I wanted to be the red cloth dangling in front of him, offering myself up for him to ravage. I wanted his muscular arms holding me down while his giant cock slammed into me until I had to beg him to stop.

Those were the messed up, twisted feels his anger gave me.

When Havoc joined us, his eyes were still wild, and his posture was rigid. A thrill went up my spine as images of him scooping me into his arms and carrying me upstairs—smacking my ass the entire way —danced through my head. Instead, he sat beside me.

A couple of his knuckles were bleeding, and he was breathing hard. I could almost taste the testosterone in the air, and it made me clench my thighs together.

"You okay?" I asked.

"Better," he replied.

"Let me get you a beer," Bull said, heading behind the bar.

I figured Havoc could use much more than a drink, though. With Emily and Bull on the other side of the bar, I slipped my hand under the hem of his T-shirt and down past the waistband of his jeans until my fingers brushed the tip of his cock. He watched me, his expression unreadable as I reached deeper, encouraged by the way he grew and hardened.

Bull slid a beer across the bar and Havoc thanked him, taking a long pull.

With my hand down his pants right there where anyone could come around the corner and see, I felt so naughty. So brazen. It made me even hornier and more desperate for him. Emily and Bull were talking about something, but all my attention was on Havoc. Leaning against him, I whispered, "You said you have a room here?"

He nodded, taking another drink. "I worry about your sense of self-preservation," he whispered.

Smiling up at him, I squeezed the head of his cock, watching him grit his teeth against the moan that wanted to escape. I squeezed harder. "What sense of self-preservation?"

"Exactly."

Precum covered the tips of my fingers, making them sticky. I pulled out my hand and turned away from the bar, so I could discreetly lick them. Havoc watched me, his eyes still dark and wild.

"I want your cock in my mouth," I whispered. "Down my throat. I want you—"

Before I could finish, he scooped his hands under my ass and hefted me over his shoulder. "We're heading upstairs," he announced.

I pressed my hands against his back, angling myself to see the room. Emily's smile was amused.

"Goodnight!" I said.

She and Bull both replied in kind as Havoc packed me up the stairs like a giant bag of flour. Once we were away from prying eyes, he smacked me on the ass. Hard. I moaned, wordlessly begging for more.

He unlocked a door, and we stepped into a small, sparse room furnished with a king-sized bed, a small dresser, and a thirty-two-inch television mounted on the wall. There were no pictures, everything was clean, and even the blankets on the bed were neutral colors.

"This is where you bring girls to screw?" I asked. I don't know why the question stumbled past my lips, but I was in shock. Havoc's house had tons of personality, and this place was just so blah.

"Brought girls," he corrected. "Before our arrangement. Now I just screw you."

He didn't take women to his house. All they ever saw of him was this shell that didn't represent him at all. Only I'd seen the real Havoc. Only I knew about the family photos lining his hallway, had heard the stories about his sisters, had perused his video collection, and knew which radio station he listened to in the morning. Only me. Something about that both thrilled and terrified me. Before I could evaluate either emotion to decide which was predominant, Havoc unzipped his pants and let his dick spring free.

"Speaking of which, I believe you were saying something about where I should put my cock...?" he asked, watching me in that all-knowing way he had about him. I knew he'd picked up on both my emotions and was offering the distraction to help pull me out of my mind.

It was crazy, the way he always seemed to know what I needed. I fell to my knees in front of him and licked him from balls to tip. He shuddered, so I did it again, smiling up at him.

"Think it's wise to tease me?" he asked.

"I think it's fun."

His hands framed my face and lifted my chin. "This is more than fun, Jules."

He was so damn intense that my entire body heated, and my heart ached. I wasn't ready to go there. Wasn't ready to be more than friends with benefits, regardless of how good those benefits were. Needing to keep things light, friendly, I licked him again. "I'm going to need you to fuck my mouth now." I sucked on the tip of his cock, my gaze still locked with his.

"God, I love your filthy mouth," he said, pushing past my lips. "Especially when I'm inside it."

I cupped his balls while he slid himself in further. Deeper. Down my throat. Making me gag as I hollowed out my cheeks to take more of him in. His hand gripped the back of my head, sliding me up and down his shaft. Pushing through to the back of my throat. He picked up the pace, pumping in and out of me until he started throbbing. Then, before he could come, he pulled out of my mouth. Disappointed, I licked his tip before sliding my lips back over him.

He pulled out again and hooked his hands beneath my arms, hefting me to my feet and kissing me roughly as his hands roamed my body. When he finally released me, that feral look I craved was back in his eyes and more intense than ever.

"See, there," he growled. "If you had any sense of self-preservation, you'd be terrified."

Grinning, and excited to see his beast again, I kissed his nose. "You don't scare me. You're like a big teddy bear that likes to growl a lot, but you're all soft and mushy inside."

He lunged, and I jumped back, running to the side of his bed. While he slowly circled around like some sort of predator closing in on his prey, I kicked off my boots and yanked my shirt over my head. His gaze took in my lacy blue bra and his nostrils flared. He was upon me, so I leapt onto the bed, pressing myself against the wall as I unfastened my bra and threw it at him.

He took a swipe at me, but I backed toward the other side of the bed. "What?" I asked, sticking out my chest. I palmed my breasts and flicking my thumbs over the nipples. "Do you want to touch these? To play with them? They feel fantastic. I bet you'd like them."

Growling, he reached for me again, but I jumped down, putting the bed between us. Unfastening my jeans, I shimmied out of them and took off my socks while keeping both eyes on Havoc. All that was left was my lacy blue thong.

"See something you like?" I asked, turning around to give him the three-sixty view. "Something you'd like to spank?" I swatted myself on the ass. Then I bent over and grabbed my ankles, looking at him between my legs. "Something you'd like to fuck?"

He was like a blur, leaping over the bed toward me. I righted myself while trying to vault out of the way, but lost my balance. I would have fallen, but Havoc had me trapped in his arms. He tossed me onto the bed, then tugged his shirt over his head and used it to bind my hands to the headboard. Halfheartedly, I struggled against my bonds as the excitement of being restrained sent more waves of heat to my core.

"You're not going anywhere," he said, his gaze raking over my body. "Not until I'm good and done with you." He dropped his pants and stroked his cock a few times while watching my writhing body. Climbing up the foot of the bed, he stopped between my legs and grinned. "Your panties are soaked, and I can smell your desire. You want me so fuckin' bad right now, don't you?"

I nodded.

"Good." He grinned, lowering his lips to right above my center. "This will be fun."

He rubbed me through my lace thong, and the sensation almost drove me over the edge. When I was close, he pushed aside the thin fabric and licked at my folds. "You taste so good, Jules." He dipped his tongue into my pussy. "So fuckin' good. I could eat you every day. I just might."

Restrained, I had no choice but to let him tease me. Every time I was about to come, he'd back off and play with my nipples, or rub his cock between my folds. He held back, teasing, playing, driving me insane as I fought to get free.

"What will you do if I let you go?" he asked.

I didn't even have to think about the answer, because I'd been fantasizing about it for the past ten minutes. "I'll grab your head and hold your mouth to my pussy until you make me come."

His eyes widened. "You dirty little tramp. Use your legs." Then he started tongue-fucking me again.

His words sank in, and I did exactly that, bending my knees and using my feet to press against the back of his head. I held him there until he finally licked me hard enough to release the dam of pleasure that had been building since he'd started. Afterward, while I was floating in an orgasmic cloud of amazingness, he piled pillows under my ass, raising me up to where he wanted me. Then he hooked my ankles behind his head and plowed into me.

"Fuck!" I shouted.

He was so deep, and I was still coming down from the last high he'd given me. He rubbed slowly against all my sensitive areas, and it took everything in me not to scream. Not to beg him for more. Leaning down, he popped one nipple in his mouth, sucking and nipping while he pinched the other. It hurt so good, I wanted more. He took me to the edge again, and then pulled out long enough to unhook my hands and flip me over onto my knees. He buried two fingers inside of me and slapped my ass hard as he attacked my g-spot. I saw stars. Another slap. I was coming so hard, squeezing his fingers so tightly, I thought I was going to burst. Another slap.

"You like that?" he asked.

Slap.

"Want me to keep doing it?"

Slap.

"Yes!" I shouted. "God, I'm still coming!"

He chuckled, slapping me again.

My ears were ringing. The room was spinning. My arms felt like Jell-O. I collapsed, but my ass was still in the air thanks to the pillows stacked beneath my hips. Havoc shoved the pillows out of the way and flipped me back over onto my back.

"There." He smiled down at me as he settled himself between my legs, pressing the tip of his cock against my center. "I want you watching me when I come."

Which was all very sweet, but my eyes were so damn heavy they kept trying to close.

"Jules," he said, pinching my nipple.

My eyes snapped open. "Ouch."

"Stay with me. I need you here with me."

He spread my legs and buried himself inside me again. My eyes wanted to roll back in my head, but I forced them to stay open. To stay focused on Havoc. He smiled. "You are so fuckin' beautiful. So fuckin' perfect. I know you're not ready to hear it, but this thing between us... this is more than friendship, Jules. This is the real deal, and I need your fine ass wearing my property patch, so I don't have to kill my motherfuckin' brothers."

My heart clenched, and my eyes burned. I wanted to be with Havoc, but I didn't know if I was ready for that yet. We'd only known each other a couple of weeks, after all.

"I have trust issues," I said.

He quirked a smile at me "I'm aware."

"Especially with men."

He was still slowly sliding in and out of me, and despite my exhaustion and euphoria, I headed toward another climax. The way he could work my body was awe-inspiring.

"But not with me," he said.

"Why do you think that is?"

His smiled widened as he thrust into me harder, deeper. "Isn't it obvious, babe? You've never met a man like me before."

I lacked the breath to tell him how ridiculous and corny he sounded. He gave up on the slow and easy bit and picked up his pace, pounding into me like a man possessed. As our gazes stayed locked, and his body continued to drive mine toward the edge, I had to admit that he was right. I never had met a man like him before. I just hoped he didn't turn out to be like all the rest of them.

17

Julia

MONDAY MORNING, HAVOC parked in the back of my bookstore, just like he'd been doing for the past four days. Five glorious nights in his bed, with the promise of many more to come, had made me hopeful about the future, despite Wesley's threat. I'd crunched numbers yesterday and discovered that between the money in my bank account and what I could pull from my investments, I could keep the bookstore open for six months. Seven if I stopped eating. If I let Justine go immediately, I could extend the date further, but I was still trying to figure out a way around screwing up her life, too.

I planned to break the news and keep her employed while she searched for a new job.

Climbing off Havoc's bike, I removed my helmet, sticking it in his saddle bag as Stocks parked beside us. Still dreading the talk with my one and only employee, I unlocked the store. Havoc slid past me to scope out the space and make sure it was clear, leaving me outside in the cool morning air with Stocks. Stocks was apparently going to be my bodyguard, and you'd think I was the queen of England with the way he kept his head on a swivel, watching all directions at once as if expecting an all-out invasion.

"It's not a dangerous neighborhood," I said, reassuringly.

He didn't look convinced.

Deciding I should get to know him, I asked, "How long have you been out of the service?"

"About a year and a half."

"Are you packing?" I don't know what made me ask, but it seemed like something I should know about my bodyguard.

Stocks shook his head. "No weapons. I'm on probation."

Awesome. Before I could ask what he'd been convicted of, earning said probation, Havoc reappeared to give us the all clear. Stocks marched into the store while Havoc held me back to give me a passionate, panty-melting kiss.

"Be careful," he said, squeezing me against him. "Call me if anything happens."

"You know I work at a bookstore, right?" I asked. "The most danger I've seen was when you were making books crash around me."

He grinned. "That was fun. We should do it again soon."

That sounded like a fantastic idea. I matched his grin, backing into the store. "I still have two more chairs we can break."

He chuckled. "Challenge accepted."

Oh boy.

He watched as I locked the barred glass door behind me, and then I watched his nice ass walk away. He swung one leg over his bike, gave me a smirk, slipped his helmet on, and motored off. I stared after him, wondering how that smirk made my chest flutter every stinkin' time he flashed it. He turned out of the parking lot, and I was no closer to solving the mystery, so I pushed off the door and headed into the break room to start coffee. While the pot was brewing, I unlocked the store, turned on all the lights, and flipped the sign to open.

"How do you like your coffee?" I asked Stocks on my way back into the break room.

"Black," he replied, settling into position beside the big storefront windows where he had a good view of both the street and the store, clearly taking this guard duty gig pretty seriously.

Trying not to roll my eyes at his unnecessary commitment, I dipped back into the break room to pour our coffees then carried them both out to the counter. Stocks stepped forward to accept his, thanking me, and I took my place behind the counter. We sipped in silence for a moment as he watched the street and I watched him.

"How long have you known Havoc?" I asked.

"A few months. Met him in the slammer."

I wouldn't have pegged Stocks for a convict. From his short, dark hair to his clean-shaven face, to his perfect posture and hardened eyes, he looked like a soldier or a cop. Maybe a firefighter. I couldn't help but wonder what he'd done to get locked up. I was trying not to pry, but he wasn't exactly the sharing type and my curiosity was one hell of a nosy bitch.

Finally, I couldn't take it anymore. "What were you locked up for?" I asked.

"Work incident."

My eyebrows rose. "What was the charge?"

I didn't think he was going to answer me, but he relented. "Destruction of private property and aggravated assault."

"So, you lost your temper at work." I shrugged. "Happens to the best of us. So... give me some details."

He didn't reply.

"Come on. I'm with Havoc. It's not like I'm gonna judge you for losing your shit."

He shook his head, chuckling. "Anybody ever tell you you're relentless?"

"No. They usually use the word nosy. I've also been rightfully accused of meddling."

Grinning, he said, "Havoc could use some meddling, the tight-lipped motherfucker."

I cocked my head to the side, wondering if we knew the same Havoc. He didn't blab or gossip or anything annoying like that, but Havoc and I spoke plenty, and he sure as hell never brushed off my questions like Stocks was attempting to do.

Before I could ask Stocks what he meant, my cell dinged with an incoming text. I pulled it out of my purse and thumbed it on. Another unknown number.

'Times up, Julia.'

I'd known he was going to contact me, but it still

took the wind out of my sails. My shoulders tensed and I braced, waiting for something bad to happen. For the ground to open up and swallow me whole, for a meteor to fall from the sky, something.

"Everything okay?" Stocks asked.

I forced a smile. "Peachy."

My phone stayed silent. Knowing the anticipation would drive me crazy if I didn't do something, I tried to take my mind off it by starting up my computer and running a report on the upcoming new book releases. I was about halfway through placing my weekly order when the door rang, announcing customers. Stocks greeted the elderly couple who came in, somehow managing to turn off his scary military biker persona with a welcoming smile. They asked for the non-fiction section and he looked to me.

"Right this way," I said, stepping around the counter to lead them.

Once they were situated and browsing, I returned and checked my phone again. Still no new texts from Wesley.

The weekend was over, and I'd lose the payments from my trust fund. I was losing my only real means of financial support. What else did the diseased ass moth have in store for me? *Forget it.* Refusing to worry about Wesley's devious plans, I opened a browser on my computer and started searching out ways to make money.

Maybe a night job?

I scanned other options, but the thought kept crossing my mind, sounding more and more appealing. Who needed sleep anyway? Not this girl. Not while I had coffee. Besides, I could nap while running the bookstore if I needed to. Especially with Stocks guarding the door.

More customers came in. A mom and her two young daughters. I left them in the children's section and went back to my computer to search local help wanted ads. I could tend bar or wait tables. Of course, both jobs required certifications and that would take time and money to acquire. The food server certification looked simple, though. I could do that. Easy peasy. Now, I just needed a restaurant that would hire me with absolutely no serving experience.

Maybe serving the homeless would count as experience? I'd gotten a whopping five hours of volunteer work under my belt... I could prepare a résumé around that shit.

The bell over the door chimed again. Thinking we were unusually busy for a Monday morning, I looked up to find a courier holding an envelope.

"Julia Edwards?" he asked, approaching.

"Yes?"

Stocks stepped between us.

The courier looked from me to stocks, then back to me. "I have a certified letter for you." He held it up. "Just need your signature."

I circled the counter to stand beside Stocks.

Gaze remaining on Stocks, the courier held an electronic tablet out to me. "Sign here, please."

I signed with my finger and he glanced at my signature before passing me the envelope with a quiet thanks. He turned and was out of the door before I even had the chance to read the name of the sender.

"Is everything okay?" Stocks asked, eyeing the envelope cradled in my hands.

"I don't know. It's from my landlady." I peeled away the easy-open strip as an uneasy feeling tightened around me. I knew in the pit of my stomach that this was what I'd been waiting for. The other shoe was dropping. I pulled out the pages and started reading. A two-page eviction notice. How could my world turn upside down with two pages? This wasn't a shoe; it was a giant anvil that would crush me. My sweet little landlady, Mary Jeeters, had given me twenty days to vacate the premises.

"Julia?" Stocks asked, watching me.

"I have twenty days." My voice sounded strange, as if someone else was speaking. Someone whose heart wasn't breaking as she read over the notice details. Someone who wasn't about to lose everything she loved. Twenty days to find a new lease and pay for a move? Impossible. Not even a night job could save me now.

"The building wasn't for sale. Mary promised to tell me if she ever decided to sell."

"Something must have changed," Stocks said.

Yep, and I had a sinking feeling I knew just who that something was. Needing to confirm my suspicions, I called Mary directly.

"Oh, honey, isn't it wonderful?" she gushed, making no sense whatsoever. "Such a sweet gesture. So romantic, I couldn't say no. Especially not at the price he was offering."

"What gesture?" I asked, rubbing my temples, trying to ease away the migraine that was building.

"He hasn't told you yet? Oh, dear, I don't want to ruin the surprise."

"Surprise? I received your letter and I'm having a heart attack here, trying to figure out how I'm going to move in twenty days."

"He was supposed to tell you this weekend."

Frustrated, I asked, "Who? Tell me what?"

"Your fiancé bought the building as an engagement gift for you. He's having you move out, so he can renovate your store and apartment. Make it trendier. He wrote it into the terms of the contract. Oh, I do hope I didn't spoil the surprise, but he's such a sweet young man I know he wouldn't want you to worry. He obviously loves you dearly."

Fucking Wesley.

Sweet man. Loved me dearly.

I couldn't breathe. My chest hurt, and my pulse raced, and the kindness and excitement in her voice were far too much for me to handle.

"Thank you, Mary." I managed to choke out. "Goodbye."

Hanging up, I lowered my head to my arms and fought the urge to cry. I'd known he was going to do something, but I hadn't braced for this. How could I?

"Julia?" Stocks asked. "Should I call Havoc?"

"Not yet. Give me a minute."

I had one place in the world that I could call home, and that immoral, merciless mangina planned to take it from me. I'd kill him. I'd stab him in the chest and rip out his cold, dead heart. Desperate to rally potential allies, I tried Laura again. Her phone went straight to voicemail.

Fucking honeymoon!

With no other options, I did the unthinkable and called my father. Surprisingly enough, he took my call.

"Julia." His tone was clipped. Guarded. "It's nice to hear from you."

"Is it, Dad?" I asked, my sadness and fear churning to anger. "Is it really?"

"My hands are tied. You know about the stipulations on the—"

"He's taking my bookstore." I blurted out. "My apartment. Everything. He purchased the building and served me an eviction notice."

Dad let out a breath. "I was hoping he wouldn't give you that ultimatum. I tried to talk to him, but Wesley hasn't been the same since you left. Since the wedding, he's been erratic and unpredictable. I think seeing you with another man affected him more than any of us thought it would. He wants you back, and you know he won't take no for an answer. He's pressed me to cut off your trust fund payments, and without them, you won't have the means to fight him."

"You *could* change the stipulations on the trust fund," I reminded him. "Your hands *aren't* tied. Not really."

"But the business, Julia. You know I can't do that. Be reasonable."

My heart sank. I scanned the bookstore—the sweet elderly couple perusing the nonfiction section, the mom reading to her two daughters in the children's section—this was my life. I refused to let Wesley or my father's business take it away. "I've never asked you for anything. Not once."

"I know," he huffed. "But this... We've been fostering this relationship for decades."

"And this is my store. My livelihood. My life."

"Wesley assured me he'll let you keep the store. Please see reason and return to your husband, Julia."

See reason? "He's not my husband," I growled. I'd tried talking, begging, and now I only had one card left. I slipped away from the ears of my customers and into the break room to play. "Did you know Wesley was in cahoots with the Kinlans?" I asked.

Dad drew in a sharp breath. "Cahoots? That is a dangerous accusation to make. Especially over the phone."

I snorted. "He's about to take everything from me, and you think I care about exposing him? They found teenage girls in one of those warehouses. Teenage girls being trafficked."

"I read the report."

"Wesley's involvement. Did. You. Know?"

His silence was more than enough of an answer. Disgusted, I shook my head. My eyes burned, and it felt like the room was caving in on me, like my entire world was crumbling around me. "Oh, God, were you and Mom part of it, too?"

"No."

He wouldn't tell me even if they had been. My stomach cramped. The back of my throat felt raw. Did I even know these people? "But that's the type of man you want me married to? Someone who traffics teenage girls."

"We all make mistakes in business, Julia. Do not pretend to be clean and righteous. I know you. I know the things you've done."

"Things I did for *you!*" A sob escaped from my throat. Taking a deep breath to settle myself, I said, "Do you know why I was content to be Mom's puppet? To be your bargaining chip?"

"Don't act like you got nothing out of the deal. Your trust fund—"

"Fuck my trust fund. You and Mom have dangled it over my head long enough, but you know what? The trust fund didn't pull my strings. You guys did. I danced for you. For your approval and respect. I don't give a flying fuck about the money." Tears were streaming down my cheeks. I angrily brushed them away. "All I ever wanted was to make you proud—to make you love me—and all you ever cared about was your business, your name, and your goddamn reputation."

"Julia—"

"No. You call Wesley and you let him know that I'm never coming back to him. And if he takes away my store, I swear I will attack him with everything I have. I will call everyone who will listen and tell them he was in bed with the Kinlans. That he's probably the one who had them murdered."

"You have no proof, and he will—"

"I don't care. This is my chess game now, and I'd rather sacrifice myself than let him win."

"Julia, listen to reason."

"Again, with the reason? I'm so sick and tired of

listening to your stupid reasoning. I'm not your fucking puppet anymore, Dad. Consider the strings cut."

I ended the call.

So much emotion flooded me. Relief. Failure. Sorrow. Anger. It was too much to handle. Too much to even decipher. My cheeks were wet, my heart was broken, and not only had I cut ties to my family, but I'd burned the strings.

What would happen when Laura came back? Would she be allowed to see me, or would they take her away, too?

I needed pills and the Nā Pali Coastline. I needed to shove these feelings away so I could think. There had to be something I could do.

"Julia?" Stocks said from the doorway, his tone concerned. "I hate to bother you, but the couple out here wants to ring up their purchase. If you could show me how to use the cash register..."

I took a deep breath and wiped my cheeks. Then I pasted a smile on my face and went to go ring up my customers.

The young family left shortly after the elderly couple. When everyone was gone, I called Havoc and filled him in on the situation.

"What are you going to do?" he asked.

"The less you know, the better," I replied.

"Jules..."

I leaned against the counter. "Thought I'd drive over to his house, light a match, and see what happens. Let it work itself out."

"Arson? You really want to go down like that?" He was trying to keep things light, to make me feel better, but I could hear the worry in his voice. It touched something deep inside me.

"Not really, but I could probably get off on a second-degree charge. We're talking a ten-year max sentence, but since I have no prior record, I'd more likely get three to nine months. I'd prefer to snap his puny little weasel neck, but murder is a trickier charge."

"I see you've been doing your homework."

"I'm nothing if not thorough."

"Babe." Havoc sighed. "I'm sorry all this shit is happening to you."

"Not your fault."

"Yeah, but I should be there for you. I need to be there for you. I'll call Brick and see if I can't get him to cover for me, so I can head over there."

Havoc was such a great guy, and I didn't deserve him at all. Dropping my head to my hands, I replied. "That's not necessary."

"I know it's not, but I also know you need me. I'll be there as soon as I can."

As much as I wanted to argue, I needed Havoc. I needed him to wrap his big warm arms around me and assure me everything would be okay. I needed his brain to help me work out a plan, his strength to keep my head up until we figured this out.

"Anything I can do?" Stocks asked, reminding me that although Havoc wasn't here, I wasn't alone.

I stood tall and let my training kick in, wrestling my emotions under control. "I'm fine, thank you," I lied. "Actually, if you could get me a bottle of water from the fridge in the break room, that'd be great."

He nodded and left, graciously giving me time to

pull myself together. I had no delusions about my parents being saints, but even if they hadn't been involved in the Kinlan's crimes, they'd known about them. They knew Wesley was involved, and they wanted me to go back to him. They would force me back into the arms of that evil son-of-a-bitch to protect their precious business.

I'd rather rip off each of my fingernails and jam them into my eyes than live with him. I'd rather have the skin flayed from my body for a purse than climb back into bed with that devil.

As I was thinking of all the other things I'd rather do, the bell above the door chimed, and Satan himself walked in.

18

Julia

WESLEY'S EYES WERE different. Dilated. Peculiar. Crazed. His top lip curled up in a sneer as he marched toward me with heavy steps, his gait purposeful. I had to fight the urge to step back. Way back. In fact, I wanted to run and hide. The instinct felt foreign and strange since I'd never been afraid of him physically. My breath hitched, and my pulse quickened.

"Wh-what are you doing here?" I asked, angry at the way my voice wavered. I cleared my throat. "You're not welcome in my story, Wesley."

"Julia?" Stocks asked, stepping into the room. His gaze shifted to Wesley. "Is everything okay?"

"Another one?" Wesley asked with a chuckle. "You sure like to slum with the biker trash, don't you, you dirty little slut?"

"Hey!" Stocks shouted, approaching. "You don't talk to her like that, motherfucker."

"Stay back," Wesley warned.

Stocks kept coming. He made it three steps before a loud THWACK rang out. He dropped my water bottle. As it rolled across the floor, Stocks's expression twisted with pain and his hands went to his stomach. "You son-of-a-bitch," he said.

My heart leaped into my throat as I tried to figure out what had happened.

Wesley was holding a pistol with a silencer attached, pointing it at Stocks. I stared from the weapon to my bodyguard, unable to believe my eyes. Stocks wobbled and leaned against the counter. Keeping one hand on his stomach, he used the other to pull himself down the counter toward Wesley.

"You want another one?" Wesley asked. "Just keep coming."

"No!" I shouted, easing toward my ex with my hands up in surrender. "No. Please, Wesley. He's... You... Stay there, Stocks. Don't come any closer. What... what do you want, Wesley? Why are you here?"

"Isn't it obvious?" he asked. "I came for what's mine." His gaze raked over my body, making me feel woozy and vulnerable. Or maybe that feeling came from the fact he was holding a gun and had just shot Stocks. "For what's always been mine."

I wanted to argue, to scream, to tell him to go jump into the Puget Sound and swim until he reached China, but the gun in his hand, and the look in his eyes, silenced me. Swallowing past my suddenly dry throat, I kept my mouth shut.

"You thought you could threaten me into leaving you alone, but you forget that nobody knows you like I do. I know what you really want. You showed me the way you like to be treated, the way you like to be fucked. You let that filthy biker fuck you like a prostitute, and you loved it. Why didn't you ever tell me that's what you wanted? That you wanted me in charge. In control. I get it now, Julia. You thought I was a pussy—that I wasn't man enough for you—but let me reassure you, I am." He gestured with the pistol toward Stocks. "Need another demonstration?"

My stomach clenched. "No. Please. I can see that you're not a pussy now. You've proven it." I needed to get him away from Stocks before he did more damage. "You came for what's yours? Fine. Take me."

"Julia, no," Stocks argued, his voice weak. He was leaning heavily on the counter as blood coated the fingers covering his wound. I wanted to go to him and stop the bleeding, but knew that would be a bad idea. The merciless look in Wesley's eyes left little doubt about what would happen if I showed Stocks compassion.

"Who the hell are you to her?" Wesley asked him.

"Nobody. He means nothing to me." I reluctantly closed the last of the distance between me and Wesley, settling my hand on his arm while my heart tried to pound out of my chest and my stomach roiled. "Just a bodyguard, and obviously not a good one, since he couldn't protect me. You're right. This whole thing with the biker was a test. I wanted you to man up and show me how savage you could be. I like it rough."

Knees knocking, lips dry, I hoped I looked more convincing than I felt.

Wesley stared at me.

From the corner of my eye, I could see Stocks. The color was draining from his face, but he was still trying to move forward. To stop Wesley. He'd die, and I couldn't let that happen.

Swallowing back bile, I leaned in and kissed Wesley's cheek. Then I whispered in his ear, "Now take me home and show me how rough you can get."

I knew I was signing my death warrant. Wesley would attempt to take me up on my offer, and I would die before I let him. Desire flared his nostrils and darkened his eyes as he wrapped an arm around my waist and tucked his gun inside his jacket.

Relieved that he'd put the weapon away, I let out a breath.

But then the barrel of the silencer dug into my side, forcing a gasp out of me. "It's not that I don't trust you, *Jules*, but if you try anything, I'll kill you and then come back to finish him off. In fact... wait. We can't leave him like this. You know better than that. What's that you always said about leaving loose ends?"

"Not murder," I argued. "This is different. I never killed anyone."

"But you want to see what a badass I can be." He leveled the pistol at Stocks once again.

His finger landed on the trigger, and I had to do something. No time to think, I shoved his arm away. There was another loud THWACK, but the shot went wide, hitting one of my bookshelves. Before Wesley could recover, I grabbed for the gun and kneed him in the balls.

"Fuck!" he shouted.

I pulled my leg up to do it again.

With his attention torn between protecting his junk and wrestling with me for his weapon, his grip was weak. I dug my fingernails into his wrists, and he cried out and backhanded me with his other hand. My face stung, my vision blurred, and stars danced before my eyes. My grip loosened, and he almost got the gun away from me.

But now I was really pissed. I gave him another hard knee to the crotch.

"Stupid bitch!" he shouted, trying to block my attacks.

My nails dug into his wrist again.

"Shit! Fuck! Stop that!"

I dug in harder. His grip on the gun loosened, and I tugged it free. Taking one big step back, placing myself between Wesley and Stocks, I leveled the gun at my ex. Eyeing me with a mixture of hate and lust, he raised his hands in the air.

"Easy, Julia. You know I wouldn't have hurt you."

"I don't know shit about you anymore. You were sex-trafficking teenage girls, you bastard. You lied to me about that note in your briefcase. The one you said was about strippers for some out-of-town clients."

His expression hardened. "You should have kept your nose out of my shit. All of this could have been prevented."

"But then I'd still be married to a fucking monster. No thanks." Unwilling to take my eyes off Wesley, I scooted to the side, so I could better see Stocks in my peripheral. "How you holding up, Stocks? Is there something I can do to stop the blood flow?"

"I need an ambulance."

And I could hear sirens closing in on our building. "They're on the way," I replied, hoping I sounded surer than I felt. "Morse put up cameras in here and he's monitoring the place. I'm sure those sirens are coming for you. Just hold on, okay?"

"They won't be in time," Wesley said. "He'll be dead, and you and I will be long gone before they arrive."

The insinuation that he would somehow regain control of the situation made my skin crawl and my finger itch to pull the trigger. His death would be so convenient, solving all my problems. I'd have access to my trust fund again. Nobody would purchase my building. I could even go back to the house we'd shared and collect all the possessions I'd abandoned in my haste to flee from the sleaze ball.

And as for letting him live... there were no real benefits to that.

I released a breath and took aim, steadying my arm. This time, I wouldn't miss.

Havoc's voice flooded my mind, reminding me I was no longer this person. That I was better. He believed in me. He trusted me. I wanted to be the woman he thought I could be.

But if I let Wesley live, he'd never give up. He'd take everything from me. What if next time he shot Havoc?

Stocks's legs gave out, and he slid down the counter to the floor, his eyes closing.

"Stocks!" I shouted.

He mumbled something incoherent.

"Clock's tickin' on that one," Wesley said with an unconcerned shrug. "Better get him the help before he bleeds out."

That's what Wesley wanted. He wanted to divert my attention so he could get the gun. I was sure of it, because that's exactly what I would do if our roles were reversed.

The sirens were getting closer.

I didn't know what to do. I took another step toward Stocks, but Wesley followed me.

"Stay back!" I shouted, waving the gun at him.

My arm was shaking, probably from holding the weapon outstretched for so long.

"Stocks," I said, nudging him with my foot. "How you doing, buddy?"

Wesley leaped at me, scowling as his arms flailed for the gun.

I couldn't let him get it. I fired. He grabbed my hands. I fired again. His face twisted in pain and his grip loosened. I fired again. He stumbled back, grabbing his chest, his expression disbelieving.

"You shot me."

Multiple times, and I'd do it again. Still pointing the gun at him, I said, "I told you to stay back."

Wesley crumpled to the floor. Blood seeped out of all three wounds, creating an abstract triangle in the middle of his chest. "You fucking bitch, you shot me!"

"I told you to stay back," I repeated, still watching him.

His eyes closed, and his breathing grew ragged. He was gasping for air.

Keeping the gun in hand, and one eye on Wesley, I bent and checked Stocks for a pulse. Weak, but still there. I let out a sigh of relief.

Flashing red and blue lights flooded the street in front of the bookstore.

Someone pounded on the back door.

There was a loud crash, and then Havoc was there, his eyes wide and wild. "You okay?" he asked.

Unable to speak, I nodded. Yes. I was okay. Wesley was not. I kept the gun trained on the bastard, just in case.

"It's okay," Havoc said. "Everything will be fine."

"I wasn't going to... Then he came at me, and... I had to. But I'm not sorry." A chuckle burst from my chest, and I covered my mouth, appalled. I wasn't sorry, but where the fuck had that come from?

"I get it, babe. It's okay." He crouched and checked Stocks's pulse. "I need some clean rags. Can you find me some?"

I gestured at Wesley with the gun. "What about him?"

"Put the gun on the counter. I don't think he'll be getting back up, but if he does, I'll take care of it."

As I set the gun down, Havoc wrapped one arm around me, keeping the other hand pressed against Stocks's stomach.

"It'll be all right, Jules," he reassured me. "I've got you. I'm sorry I didn't get here sooner."

Tears were racing down my face. I let out another sob, and then straightened, needing to force the strength to get through this. "I already told you, Marcus, it was my job to put that bullet in his heart."

The front door burst open, and the police rushed in, shouting at us to put our hands in the air.

19

Havoc

Two months later

"YOU GOT THE rings?" Link asked me for the fifth time in as many minutes. I wanted to tell him to get bent and carry his own goddamn rings. I had one job. Did he really think I was going to fuck it up? Still, I understood my friend was a wreck, and I couldn't fault him for coming off like a paranoid foreman on his first job. Emily was his world, and he wanted to give her the wedding she was worthy of. As Link had said, he loved her, and would do anything for her. And I would do anything for Link, which explained why I was wearing a monkey suit for the second time this year, putting up with his crazy anxiety.

"Got 'em," I said, patting one of the three things currently in my jacket pockets as I smiled to myself. Link would lose his shit if I gave him the wrong box.

"I'm sure he hasn't lost the damn rings since the

last time you asked, Prez," Wasp added, as always, having a little fun at Link's expense. "What's wrong? You having second thoughts? Ready to hock the rings and head to Vegas? You're not turning into a yellowbelly on us, are you?"

"Fuck off, Wasp," Link growled. Then he seemed to remember that there was a preacher standing beside him and apologized.

"That's quite all right," the preacher said, gesturing toward the back of the room where Link's father, Jake, was waving like a mad man. "Looks like the ladies are ready for you, though."

Wasp, Eagle, and I left Link to stand with the preacher at the front of the room. Above his head, a giant clock ticked away the minutes left of his bachelorhood. Emily had suggested the fire station for the venue, but Link had called in a favor to surprise her with a booking of the Joni Earl Great Hall at Union Station. And as I walked under the barrel-vaulted ceilings with inset lights, past the rows of padded chairs, toward the black and white mosaic dance floor, I had to give my boy mad props for pulling this shit off. Any woman who got married here would feel like a fucking queen. Emily was good people, and she deserved the best. She deserved Link.

"Can't believe he's tying the knot," Wasp said as we made the trek down the aisle. Then something caught his attention. He winked, and I followed his gaze to find a cute little brunette sitting toward the back of the room.

She rolled her eyes and looked away, low-key flipping him off in the process.

Eagle chuckled. "You better leave Carly alone before Flint kicks your ass."

"Carly?" I asked.

"Flint's new bartender. Wasp has been trying to get into her pants for months now, but she wants nothing to do with this asshole."

"She's just playing hard to get," Wasp said with a shrug. "I'll get her. You'll see."

"Your funeral," Eagle replied as we came to a stop.

I cast one more glance over my shoulder to find Link fiddling with his cuff links. I'd been in the trenches with him, literally and metaphorically, but I'd never seen him so goddamn nervous in my life. Chuckling and shaking my head, I turned to face Jake. "They're ready?"

As Link's best man, I'd be walking down the aisle with Jayson, Emily's man of honor. Not my first choice, but at least it'd be entertaining. With Jayson around, things usually were. Since it would probably kill Emily's colorful assistant to do anything normal, he'd opted out of wearing a traditional black suit, and scooted around the corner in a tight-ass emerald green getup to match the bridesmaids.

"Havoc," Jayson said, eyeing me up and down before licking his lips. "You look absolutely delicious."

Jayson's open appreciation of the male form was difficult for some of my brothers to stomach, but I was comfortable enough with my masculinity that I didn't let that shit bother me. "Thanks. You look..." What the fuck could I say? He looked like the Rid-

211

dler about to make his porn debut. He just needed a pimp hat and a cane.

"Dashing," Jayson provided, saving me from coming up with an answer. "Also acceptable are dapper, stylish, debonair, and sexy as fuck."

I chuckled, holding out my arm. Jayson took it with a shit-eating grin. "You ready to do this?" I asked.

"Watch my favorite girl start her happily ever after with a tattooed beefcake? Absolutely. I cannot wait to see Link's face when she appears. That big, bad biker is going to bawl like a baby. You might, too, you know? If you need a shoulder to cry on, you know I'll be here for you, big boy."

We started our walk. "Thanks, but Julia sees to my needs just fine."

"I bet." He waggled his eyebrows suggestively. "She's good for you. You smile a lot more when she's around. Of course, I could make your fine ass smile, too."

Still chuckling, I dropped him on Emily's side of the preacher before taking my place beside Link.

Wasp and Naomi came down the aisle next. Naomi was Link's sister, and the most badass broad I'd ever met. I'd seen her beat a man's ass with a wrench once when asked her why she thought she should work in the auto shop. Even the strapless, floor length green dress she wore couldn't soften the hard lines and angles of her body as she marched up the aisle, looking every bit the Air Force helicopter pilot she was. She'd taken leave for the wedding and the club couldn't have been happier to have her home. It had been one big party since she arrived. Even if her presence turned Eagle into a star-crossed pussy. Those two shared a complicated history that it would take a magician to unravel. But since Naomi would ship out again soon, that would have to wait.

And we'd have to deal with Eagle pining over her like a little bitch.

Wasp settled Naomi beside Jayson and then joined me and Link.

The next couple required my full attention, because Eagle had Julia on his arm. She was so gorgeous that the sight took my goddamn breath away. Hair up, dress clinging to her incredible curves, her bright green eyes locked on mine as she walked down the aisle. It took everything in me not to tug her fine ass away from Eagle. Eagle glanced at me, and then picked up the pace, hurrying Julia along. She gave me a knowing smirk as she took her place beside Naomi.

Naomi's gaze fixed on Eagle, and I was hella glad there were no wrenches within reach.

Finally, the music changed, and Emily began her walk down the aisle on the arm of Jake. Her soon-to-be father-in-law was the closest thing she had to a dad, and he'd been so goddamn over-the-moon when she'd asked him to do the honors, he hadn't shut up about it for days. Grin stretched across his face, he patted Emily's hand and dutifully marched her toward us.

A strangled sound came from Link. I looked up to find my friend tearing up as he stared at his bride. I couldn't blame him. Emily was quite the sight in her long white dress, smiling at him as her own eyes flooded with emotion. Jake kissed her cheek and offered her to Link before taking a seat beside his wife.

The ceremony was quick, but the kiss Link sealed it with wasn't. We'd packed the Great Hall with guests, and every rambunctious one of them hooted and hollered as Link dipped Emily back and attacked her mouth in front of God and all the witnesses. The preacher cleared his throat and took a step back. When Link finally let Emily up for air, they were both disheveled and panting. The preacher, no doubt in a hurry to make it legal before they consummated, presented Mr. and Mrs. Tyler Lincoln.

The wedding party was shoved together for pictures, and then it was time to cut loose.

Having plans for a different kind of party, I grabbed Julia's hand and led her away from the festivities, toward the private room the bridal party had used to get ready.

20

Havoc

"What are you doing?" Julia asked, giggling as she let me pull her away. "The party's that direction."

"I know. I got you a surprise." Locking the dressing room door behind us, I winked at her.

Her eyebrows rose at the insinuation, as her hand ran along the seam of my jacket, drifting down toward my pants. "Just what kind of surprise are you talking about here, Marcus?"

Since the shooting, she'd taken to using my given name in private, and it had never sounded better.

"You know how you said you wanted to have sex in public, but on the down low?"

Her eyes widened, and her pupils dilated. She leaned against me. "Yes?"

I tugged a small bag out of my pocket and dumped its contents into my palm. It was a curved pink vibrator designed to fit up against her g-spot with a u-shaped tail that would press against her clit and serve as an antenna. She leaned closer, getting a better view. I pressed the power button, and an internal light came on. "This goes inside of you, with this little thing against your clit. I'll use an app on my phone to remotely operate it."

Her jaw dropped in mock dismay, but her gaze stayed firmly on the toy. "It's your best friend's wedding. I can't be wearing a vibrator during it."

"The wedding's over. This is for the reception, and you know all those motherfuckers are out there getting hammered. Nobody will know what we're doing. And trust me, if Link knew, his horny ass would approve. You better believe he'd go right out and buy one for Emily. Probably already has."

The look in her eyes, and the thought of her walking around in a room full of our closest friends while I controlled her pleasure, was making me so damn hard I could barely see straight.

"Come on, babe, it'll be fun."

"Oh, I'm sure it will be." She took the vibrator from me and studied it. "So, I just stick it inside me?"

"Want me to do it?" I offered, pulling out a small bottle of lube.

She took the lube, shaking her head. "I think I can manage."

"Can I at least watch?"

She considered the question for a moment before nodding. Then, she leaned against the wall and slowly raised the hem of her dress up her long, sexy legs to her waist.

"Here, let me help you with that," I said, holding up her dress to free her hands.

"You're always so helpful," she said with a giggle.

I shrugged, eyeing her lacy white thong, anticipating removing it later. "I do what I can."

She applied the lube, then handed me back the bottle. Vibrator in one hand, she used the other to push aside her thong and slide the little pink toy inside her, its tail snaking out to settle between her folds with the tip pressing against her clit. She righted her panties and stood.

"How does that feel?" I asked, my voice low and husky. If I didn't want to fulfill her fantasy so much, I'd bend her over one of the chairs, take that thing out of her, and fuck her until neither of us could walk out of here.

"Good," she replied. "It's comfortable."

"Let's see if it works." I pulled up my phone and started the app, giving her pussy a brief pulse.

She jumped. "Yep. Works." She laughed with her hand in front of her crotch. "Can you hear it?"

"Not at all."

"Are you sure?"

I cranked up the vibration, but still couldn't hear it. Especially not with the music coming from the other side of the wall. "Nope."

Julia moaned, doubling over. "Turn it down. Turn it down!"

Laughing, I lowered the vibration.

"Ohmigod. I just realized the power you have right now. Why in the world did I agree to this?"

"Because you love me and you like trying new things with me." I grabbed her face and kissed her deeply while fiddling with the controls. She moaned into my mouth, and I turned the toy's intensity up, still holding her chin in my hand. It took less than a minute before Julia was writhing beneath my kiss as release ripped through her. I lowered the intensity and let her ride out her orgasm before turning it off completely.

"Fuck," she breathed, leaning against me for support. "Holy shit-fuck."

"Thought it would be best to get the first one out of the way, so you're not so sensitive."

She was panting. "You're going to do this to me out there?"

Nodding, I grinned. "And you might want to try to hide your reaction a little better. They're not *that* drunk yet. Let's see your game face, Jules."

Pulling away from me, she straightened her dress and took a deep breath, giving me a cool, collected smile. I'd believe she had her shit together if it weren't for her lust-filled eyes and the blush across her cheeks.

"Goddamn, you are so beautiful." Unable to help myself, I kissed her again. "I love you so damn much. I hope you know that."

Her smile heated, and her eyes softened. "I love you, too, Marcus." She took another deep breath. "Now take me out to the reception and give me numerous orgasms in the middle of everyone we know and love." She paused, as if considering what she'd just said. "We're going straight to hell. You know that, right?"

I shrugged. "Might as well have a good time along the way."

Putting her vibrator on low, I offered her my arm. She took a moment to get used to the sensation before accepting my arm. We headed out to join the crowd.

Our first stop was Stocks. I clapped my friend on the shoulder and asked, "How you feelin' brother?"

"Good." He turned to face us, giving Julia a hug. She carefully angled her body away from his. "The doc says everything's healing nicely. Should be able to ride again by next week."

The gunshot had missed his stomach but clipped his large intestine. He'd undergone a couple of surgeries and had to fight off an infection, but he was on the mend. I'd been following his progress and making sure he got the best care available. Stocks had taken a bullet while protecting my woman, and there wasn't a goddamn thing in the world I wouldn't do for him. I was already badgering Link about patching him in early. The motherfucker had earned it, if you asked me.

"You need anything, you let me know," I said, reminding him for the thousandth time since the incident that I was at his disposal.

As we walked away from Stocks, Julia joined a few of the old ladies and I fiddled with the app, turning her toy up and down in intensity, watching her reaction. Her body made little jerks, and occasionally her gaze sought me out, but mostly, she handled it like a boss.

After one particularly heavy attack on her pussy, she drifted over and gave me a tight smile. "You have no idea what you're doing to me."

I kissed her. "Yes, babe, I do. You enjoying it?"

She didn't have to answer, because the gleam in her eyes said it all. "Look, there's Morse," she said instead, changing the subject.

Morse was another man I owed the world to. He'd been monitoring Julia's store, and called me the instant Wesley showed up. Then he'd copied the surveillance footage and rounded up Emily and Link to meet us at the police station. The detectives assigned to the case watched the footage and interviewed us both. Julia confirmed she hadn't shot until Wesley attacked her, and since her story lined up with the footage, they released us and told us not to leave town. Thanks to Morse's quick thinking and quicker action, we weren't even booked, and no charges were ever filed.

As for Julia's shop, Wesley's death had put a quick halt to the purchase of her building. Since her name was still on the house she'd purchased with the asshole, the home was awarded to her. Morse and Tap had helped her search the premises and his home computer for dirt on her ex, and had found plenty. Not only was Wesley in bed with the Kinlans, he was also screwing over half of Seattle, including Julia's parents. He'd used "donations" from the Edwards to kick-start his little venture with the Kinlans, and then blackmailed them over their gift.

The dumbasses had trusted the wrong man with both their money and their daughter.

We turned everything over to the feds, and last I'd heard, they'd found a link between Wesley and the Kinlan murders. Who knew what else that sick fucker was involved in? Seattle's a hell of a lot better off with him gone.

Julia recently signed papers to sell the house she'd shared with Wesley and had already received a few offers. She was planning to use the money to buy her commercial space, so she never had to worry about another eviction notice. Knowing her parents were being blackmailed hasn't changed a damn thing between her and them. However, when the smoke cleared, her asshole of a father did the right thing and released the payments from her trust fund. She was happy and doing all right for herself, and I was damn proud of her.

We congratulated the bride and groom before making our way around the rest of the room. All the while, I played with the controls to her toy, watching her as she tried not to react every time I turned up the intensity. At one point, she turned around and bit her knuckle as another orgasm raked through her body. I think that was number three. Maybe four.

I was having a blast, and seeing her like this made my dick harder than it had ever been.

Julia turned on me, her eyes wild, her body glistening, and her face framed with curls that had come loose. She grabbed my hand and tugged me back into the dressing room, locking the door behind us.

"I have a surprise for you," she said, backing me up against the door.

"What kind of surprise?" I asked, enjoying the role reversal.

She dropped to her knees, unzipped my pants, and freed my rock-hard cock. She licked it from base to head and I let out a moan. I was so damn sensitive she wouldn't have to do much before I lost control.

"Revenge. I think I'm gonna tease you until you take this thing out of me and fuck me properly."

Her lips covered the head of my cock and I sucked in a breath. She took me deep into her throat as I played with the controls again. She moaned, and I almost shot my load down her throat. I tried to pull back, but she must have changed plans, because she grabbed my ass and encouraged me to fuck her mouth. As I pumped in and out of her, I hiked up the vibration of her toy to full blast.

We came together while the party raged next door. And when we finished, I cradled Julia in my arms, stroking the loose hair out of her face, and kissed her deeply. "I have another surprise for you," I said.

She giggled. "I don't think I can handle another one."

I kissed her forehead and squeezed her against me, before releasing her to stand on her own. Her legs were a little wobbly, but four or five orgasms in a row will do that to a person. She looked thoroughly fucked and absolutely breathtaking.

"I didn't want to do this here," I said, holding her hand. "I've been trying to figure out the perfect place... the perfect way to handle this shit, but I don't want to wait any longer." Dropping to one knee, I pulled a box from my pocket. The damn thing had been in my pocket for a week, waiting for the perfect opportunity to pop the question. My patience was shot, and I knew what I wanted.

"Marry me?" I asked.

Her eyes softened as she looked from me to the box. I popped it open to reveal the square solitaire I'd purchased for her. I didn't know shit about rings, but thankfully Emily had been available to help me pick this one out. I'd wanted to go bigger, more expensive, but Emily had insisted this was the one. As Julia silently stared at the ring, I had my doubts.

"If you don't like the ring, we can get you a different one."

No response.

My heart was in my goddamn throat. She didn't move. Didn't say shit.

"Jules?"

"The ring's perfect, but we've only known each other for a couple of months," she whispered, her gaze still locked on the box. "This is crazy."

Fuck. She was going to say no. I didn't know what to do, so I stayed there waiting like a damn imbecile.

Her gaze met mine and tears flooded her eyes. "But crazy's kind of our thing, isn't it?"

I nodded. "Yeah, we do that shit well."

"Yes." She nodded, grinning. "Yes, I'll marry you, Marcus." She gestured for me to stand. "Now, put that on my finger so I can take a picture and send it to Laura. She's going to flip."

Standing, I did exactly that, and after Julia sent her photo, I took her hand in mine, and we went out to celebrate with our friends. "I love you," I whispered, kissing her cheek.

"I love you, too." Turning to face me, she added, "You know, this is kind of fitting."

"Hmm?"

223

"Our story started with a wedding, and now, you proposed to me at one. This was the perfect time and place, love." She laced her fingers behind my head and kissed me. "And even though it sounded like a really lame line, you were right. I have never met a man like you before."

Laughing, I picked her up and carried her out into the party, so goddamn happy I thought my chest would burst.

EPILOGUE

Julia

Three Months Later

HAVOC WAS GRINNING ear-to-ear as he sat beside me and leaned back in the cozy leather seat. "This is nice. I've never flown first class before."

I gaped at him. "You flew coach?" Havoc stood almost six and a half feet tall, with biceps bigger than my thighs. The thought of all that sexy dark meat squeezing into a tiny coach seat made me cramp for him.

"Shit, after the flights we had to take to Afghanistan, coach was luxury, Jules."

"Yeah, well, not for my man. Not anymore. We will be in the air for almost eight hours, with only a short layover in Atlanta to break up the flight. I would never let you endure that kind of torture. Besides, first class gets free drinks, and I'm going to need a lot of alcohol."

After all, we were flying to Richmond, Virginia, where I would meet Havoc's five sisters who'd already made it clear what they thought of me snagging their brother. "Skinny white bitch," was the last thing I heard before Havoc had disconnected the call and hung up on Janelle, who seemed to be the spokesperson of the five.

That was before Havoc's mom, Mona, showed up on his doorstep, demanding to meet me.

Things between us had started out rocky and quickly declined from there. I'd tried my best to make a good impression, but Mona seemed determined to test my worth. It had all come to a head on the second night of her visit while Havoc was in the garage tinkering on his bike and Mona and I were cooking dinner.

Mona eyed the salad I was throwing together as she stirred the greens she was cooking. "My boy doesn't need a salad. What he needs is a woman who knows how to properly prepare his vegetables."

I'd had more than enough of her passive-aggressive onslaught of insults, so I dropped my tongs and turned to face her. "Do you have something you want to say to me?"

"I'm concerned about your relationship with my boy." She continued to stir. "Marcus has one hell of a temper, and he needs a strong woman who can handle him."

"And you don't think I'm strong enough?"

She shrugged and didn't reply.

"I would do anything in the world for that man, and he knows it," I said, frustrated because I genuinely liked Mona, and I wanted her to accept me. I'd overheard her

telling Marcus she wished he'd find a nice black woman to settle down with, and I was trying not to let her words devastate me. Hurt people hurt people, and it was clear Mona had been through some shit in her lifetime. Doubtlessly, at the hands of white people. I hated this stupid wall skin color had erected between us and was desperate to knock it down. "He deserves to be loved and respected, and I will do that better than any woman out there. I promise you that." Heat flooded my face, evidence of the fire raging within, but I was determined to control my temper. "I will make him happy. Don't you want him to be happy?"

"Of course, I do."

"Good, because Marcus is mine and I'm not letting him go. You raised an incredible man, and I have nothing but respect and gratitude for you and your role in his life. But he fought for me when no one else would. I will fight for him."

Havoc must have entered while I was speaking because he picked me up, tossing me over his shoulder and carrying me to our room. I didn't know how much of the conversation he'd heard or what his reaction would be. Suspecting he was probably upset, I prepared my defense along the way. I wouldn't apologize for my words because I wasn't sorry. Mona needed to know she couldn't come between us, especially not over something as inconsequential as skin color. Nobody on the planet was more perfect for me. His skin could be purple, green, or blue, and I'd feel the same.

Havoc closed the door and set me down in front of it. I opened my mouth to explain myself, but he didn't give me the chance. He attacked me, pressing me to the door with his body as his tongue claimed my mouth. He was *passion unleashed, stealing my breath away as his fingers undid the buttons on my jeans before shoving them down. I met his ferocity, channeling the anger that had been building into a hunger for his body. I undid his pants as he unclasped my bra and set the girls free so he could play.*

With both of us still mostly dressed and his mother just down the hall, he pulled his cock out and impaled me, pinning me to the door with a powerful thrust. A cry ripped from my throat, but he swallowed it as he pulled out and drove into me again. My back hit the door and a shudder of ecstasy went up my spine. Needing more of him, I worked one leg the rest of the way out of my jeans and straddled his waist.

Havoc grabbed my ass and hoisted me further up the door. His thrusts came faster now, harder. We were both panting and nipping at each other as we chased our wild, uninhibited release. We were primal, raw, and out of control.

That was the last time Mona had taken a jab at me. After that, our relationship made a U-turn. She was pleasant, funny even, as she shared stories of Havoc's childhood antics that had him shaking his head and me roaring with laughter. By the time we put her on a plane and sent her home, I was sorry to see her go.

But that had been months ago, and people change.

What if she hated me again?

There was no way in hell I was letting Havoc go, so I used the flight to mentally prepare, just in case.

Despite several cocktails, I slept little on the flight. Worrying about his sisters, and wondering what to expect, at least a hundred scenarios filtered through my mind, most of which keyed me up and made me angry. If they started trouble—if they said anything —I'd show them a skinny white bitch. Who talked like that about someone they didn't even know, anyway? What happened to giving a person a chance? Why would they judge me before they met me?

Why did I agree to come on this trip?

Havoc, the man who'd battled my demons alongside me, snored faintly in the next seat, reminding me why I was here. I told his mom I'd do anything for him, and I meant it. Even though he hadn't said as much, I knew this visit was important to him. I had to get along with his sisters. Silently vowing to win them over, I went over all the information he'd given me about them before telling me to stop worrying and falling asleep.

How could I sleep? I was about to step into potentially hostile territory. My stomach twisted in knots as I wondered if we should stop off somewhere and buy them all gifts. No. That's what the old Julia would do. I had to find a better way.

After we landed, Havoc texted Janelle to let her know we'd arrived, and we headed down to baggage claim to wait. A little blue-haired lady wobbled over to us and stared up at Havoc, her eyes wide, reminding me of Aunt Martha's initial reaction to him. But rather than curiosity and lust, this woman gazed at Havoc with awe and respect.

"You're one of those body builders, aren't you?" she asked. Her question seemed to stun Havoc, and before he could answer, she continued, "My late husband was a bodybuilder for years. Mind you, he wasn't nearly as big as you are. I don't think I've ever seen muscles as big as yours before. Maybe on the television set. Even after he retired, my Benjamin still watched the competitions, rooting on his favorites. You wouldn't mind giving me your autograph, would you? I like to go every Sunday and visit his grave so we can chat, and I'd love to tell him all about meeting you."

Havoc didn't hesitate. "Of course. Do you have paper and a pen?"

As she dug through her purse, he gave me a sheepish smile. He wasn't a bodybuilder, at least not officially, but he sure looked the part. And if it made some little old lady happy to think he was, he'd let her believe it. My chest squeezed tight and warmth filled my veins as he signed her page and give her a hug before saying goodbye and turning back to me.

"Hey, how come you never gave me your autograph?" I asked.

He arched an eyebrow as his gaze drifted down my body. "Want me to sign with my tongue?"

Yes. I would like that very much. "You really are a good man," I said, blinking back the sting to my eyes. "A naughty, dirty, good man, but a good man nonetheless."

"I'm no saint, Jules."

"Thank God," I huffed. "I bet saints are dreadful in bed."

He laughed and tugged me in for a hug.

As we were retrieving our luggage, a group of women rushed in behind us, rustling paper as they stretched a sign in front of their faces. I tried to read it, but it rippled as they laughed, clearly cracking themselves up. Finally, they stilled enough that I could make it out.

"We're here for the lucky bastard who calls himself our brother and the woman crazy enough to marry his ugly ass."

Havoc shook his head, a smile tugging at his lips. "They're here."

The paper sign flew into the air and five gorgeous black women emerged, laughing hysterically and high-fiving one another.

"Those are your sisters?" I asked, happy to see that they at least had great senses of humor.

"Unfortunately."

"Don't even play like that, Marcus. You know you love us. Shit, if it wasn't for the five of us, you'd probably be a puny little pipsqueak, unable to bench a penny. We made you." One of the five stepped forward and hugged him before turning to face me. "Hi, Julia. I'm Erica, the youngest, smartest, and obviously best looking of the Wilson family." She hugged me.

Surprised, I patted her back and hoped I didn't look as awkward as I felt. I'd expected to get a hand shake at best, the third degree at worst. Hugs didn't fit in anywhere in my expectations.

"By 'made me' she means I had to beef up so I could defend myself. They might not look like much, but they were raised by wolves," Havoc said.

"Are you calling Mom and Daddy wolves?" another sister asked.

Havoc nodded. "Absolutely."

"Hold up. I need to set the record straight," another sister said, hugging Havoc before giving me one as well. "Erica might be the youngest, but smartest and best looking? Bitch, please. Most delusional is more like it. I'm Janelle, and I'm the one who gets shit done."

"What you need to get done is those nails. I've never seen nails so raggedy ass looking in my life," the third sister said, coming in for hugs. "I'm Tamera, by the way, and don't believe a thing that bitch says. She's the reason we were late."

"Yeah, because you spelled bastard wrong," the fourth sister added. "I'm Romona, and I'm here to warn you that Tamera can't spell worth shit."

"It was a typo," Tamera defended. "Not a spelling error. I know how to spell bastard."

"Your face is a typo," the fifth sister added. "I'm Kim, by the way. The sweet one." She batted her eyes at me and stuck a finger in her cheek, pushing in the dimple.

I'd been trying not to laugh since the introductions started, but that one did me in. As I lost it, Janelle stepped in the middle of the group. "Stop it. All of you. Of course we had to redo the sign, Tamera. Julia is our one shot at getting Marcus married off and out of our hair, and we cannot screw this up. She owns a bookstore, so we can't let her know that illiteracy runs in the family until after they tie the knot. Now stop acting like savages and be the fucking ladies Mom raised."

At that, everyone lost it. The entire group dissolved into laughter, except Havoc. He just stood back and watched us, shaking his head. "It's gonna be a long ass weekend," he muttered.

"Oh, stop being a little bitch," Kim said, tugging a set of keys out of her pocket and holding them out to him. "You don't even have to put up with us for a while. Mom's waiting for you in my car. It's parked on the fifth floor in the E section. She said to call her cell phone if you get lost."

"And what about you all?" Havoc asked, eyeing his sisters skeptically.

"Still a nosy bastard, aren't you?" Romona asked.

"I wouldn't have to be if you all weren't so damn shady."

Janelle huffed. "If you must know, we're taking our soon-to-be sister out for a spa day to relax. I'm sure she needs a little R and R after putting up with your ass across the country. You go mind your business and visit with Mom."

Havoc's gaze cut to me. "I don't know if that's a good idea."

"Look," Tamera said. "I know we made a bad first impression on your girl here, but we want to make it right. Mom said she's cool, and if she can make it past that old bat, you don't have nothing to worry about."

"Go," I assured him. If his sisters were anything like his mom, they needed to see my strength. Besides, I was looking forward to getting to know them now that I'd seen their goofy sides. "I'll be fine."

He didn't look convinced, but he kissed me goodbye and told me to call if I needed anything.

"Don't you dare call her," Erica said. "This is a

girls' day, and your meddlin' ass needs to stay out of it."

"Don't believe any stories they tell you about me," Havoc said. "Their memory from our childhood is sketchy."

"Shoot, your memory's been sketchy since Daddy dropped you on your head." Erica made shooing gestures. "Get out of here. Go. We got shit to do and you're holding us up, Marcus."

The girls were ridiculous. Despite my travel fatigue, they had me rolling during our entire spa visit. As we were primped and primed, our hair, nails, and makeup done to perfection, they fed me story after story about Marcus, and I gobbled every one of them up. The girls had no shame and held nothing back. Like him, they were all fierce and passionate, and by the time we left the spa, my face was frozen in a perma-smile, and my heart was full.

I expected us to head to Mona's house, so I was surprised when we parked in front of what appeared to be a small white bungalow, with a professionally landscaped yard that looked like it could be on the historical register. "This is where you all grew up?" I asked, trying to imagine their large, wild family contained in such a place. I couldn't make it work in my mind.

"Sure," Janelle said, as we all piled out of her minivan.

Confused by her odd response, I followed them up a dainty brick pathway to an old oak door. It wasn't a house. The interior looked more like a small church, complete with stained glass windows.

But I didn't see any of it, because Havoc stood in

the foyer, wearing a suit, looking more nervous than I'd ever seen him. His gaze landed on me, and he let out a breath, his shoulders relaxing. Then I realized Link and Wasp were standing behind him.

Confused, I shook my head. "Is everything okay?"

Havoc hurried over to me and tugged me aside. "First, you look gorgeous, but that's nothing new. Second, my mom did a thing. I... um... she arranged this all. She... I didn't know. The guys' flight came in about an hour after ours. Emily couldn't make it. She wanted to, but her morning sickness is out of control, and the flight would have been hell. She sends her love and blessings. But if this isn't what you want, we can do it later. Back home. Or wherever. Whenever."

He was rambling. My rock was all broken up and crumbling. "Do what?" I asked, wondering what had him so rattled. "What is this?"

"Surprise! You're getting married," all five of Havoc's sisters cheered behind me.

"Wait, what?" I asked.

Havoc waved the girls away. "Again, we don't have to do this right now. I want you to be happy and I'll wait if that's what you want..."

"Your family threw us a surprise wedding?" I asked.

He nodded. "They're crazy. I tried to tell you."

My body felt weird. Emotion flared in my toes like a tiny flame flickering to life. It spread like a wildfire, up my legs, to my stomach, up my arms, engulfing my heart before it finally set my mind ablaze. His family had thrown us a surprise wedding. It was the most thoughtful, wonderful, amazing act of acceptance I'd ever heard of, and Havoc was willing to throw it all away if it didn't make me happy.

"This isn't crazy." I choked up. Swallowing, I tried again. "This is the sweetest thing ever."

Havoc's eyes widened and his shoulders relaxed as he watched me, still seemingly uncertain. "You want to get married? Today? As in right now?"

"Do I have a dress?"

He nodded. "Mom won't let me see it, but she said it's the one thing my sisters agreed on. She asked me for your dress size a while back, but I didn't know she was going to get you a wedding dress. She assured me it's gorgeous and you'll love it."

"And what about the marriage license? Isn't there a waiting period or something?"

He grinned. "Not in Virginia. No waiting period, no blood tests. She printed off a paper that we all sign and take in tomorrow and bam, it's done."

My chest squeezed tight. Just like that, I could be Mrs. Marcus "Havoc" Wilson. Within hours, really. And with none of the stressful wedding planning and trying to figure out how to invite my sister without putting her in the awkward position of keeping a secret from our parents. Having a surprise wedding I had no control of was the perfect solution. It was too good to be true. "This is crazy," I said.

"Crazy's kind of our thing," he replied.

Yeah, it was. And I wouldn't change that for the world. "I need... to go get my dress on."

It took Havoc a moment to process what I'd said,

but when he did, his eyes lit up, and a grin stretched across his face. "Is that a yes?"

He looked so damn happy that a tear of joy ran down my cheek as I nodded enthusiastically. "Yes. Of course."

He kissed me, sweetly, then passionately. Then all five of his sisters circled around us, clearing their throats until he let me up for air.

"You're fucking up her makeup," Erica complained with a sigh of exasperation. "Go. Leave us to fix this." She tugged me away toward the rest of her sisters, but I caught sight of Mona and peeled off.

"Thank you," I said, wrapping my soon-to-be mother-in-law in a hug. More tears threatened, and I didn't want to face Erica's wrath, so I blinked rapidly. "This is the kindest thing anyone has ever done for me."

"I misjudged you," she replied. "I'm glad you didn't let me push you away. You're good for my son, and it's clear you make him happy. Thank you for loving him enough to fight for him." She smiled.

"I..." There were too many emotions I couldn't put into words. Too many feelings I was struggling to get out. "Will you walk me down the aisle?"

Her face lit up. She was one of the most timelessly beautiful women I'd ever seen, and when she smiled, the entire room brightened. It was easy to see where Havoc and his sisters got their good looks from. "I'd be honored."

That's how I found myself standing at the altar in a long white gown that I never would have selected for myself but looked incredible in, staring into the eyes of the "Helper of Seattle" as we were surrounded by family who supported and accepted our relationship.

I was exhausted, emotional, overwhelmed, and it was the best day of my life.

My heart felt like it was in danger of bursting as Havoc dipped me for a long, passionate kiss before picking me up and carrying me down the aisle as his sisters and club brothers hooted and hollered.

Crazy looked damn good on us.

ALSO BY HARLEY STONE

Thank you so much for reading *Wreaking Havoc*. I hope you've enjoyed Havoc and Julia's crazy story. Find out what happens next when pretty boy player Wasp falls for a single mom with a deadly secret. Get *Trapping Wasp* now.

Let's stay connected. Sign up to receive updates, new releases, and sales via my newsletter on my website at harleystoneauthor.com or in my Facebook reader group, Harley's Harem.

Also, be sure to check out my other books:

ABOUT THE AUTHOR

International bestselling author Harley Stone specializes in imperfect characters, realistic story-lines, scorching hot sex scenes, and fun, witty dialogue. She's always up for a good adventure (real or fictional), and when she's not building or reading about imaginary worlds, you can find her gallivanting with the man of her dreams.

ACKNOWLEDGMENTS

This book would have never become a reality without the help and support of so many people. Special thanks to my husband, Meltarrus, our boys, and all my friends and family for letting me off the hook when I daydreamed storyline and dialog during our conversations.

Huge thanks to the incredible Gail Goldie, who saw this first and saved the rest of the world from having to read most of my mistakes. Also, thanks to my fabulous friend KA Ware for her content edits, suggestions, and encouragement. Thank you, beta and ARC readers for your edits, support, and love.

And, thank you, reader, for embarking on this journey with me!

Made in the USA
Monee, IL
17 July 2025